William Henry Giles Kingston

The Boy who Sailed with Blake and the Orphans

William Henry Giles Kingston

The Boy who Sailed with Blake and the Orphans

ISBN/EAN: 9783337389628

Printed in Europe, USA, Canada, Australia, Japan

Cover: Foto ©Andreas Hilbeck / pixelio.de

More available books at **www.hansebooks.com**

THE VISIT TO MUSTAPHA'S HOUSE. (p. 172.)

THE BOY
WHO SAILED WITH BLAKE;

AND

THE ORPHANS.

BY

WILLIAM H. G. KINGSTON,

Author of " Charley Laurel," " The True Hero," &c.

LONDON:
SUNDAY SCHOOL UNION, 56, OLD BAILEY, E.C.

1880.

PRINTED BY

W. H. AND L. COLLINGRIDGE, CITY PRESS,

154, ALDERSGATE STREET, E.C.

PREFACE.

I T is with a mournful satisfaction that this volume is issued, containing the last story the lamented author wrote for the Sunday School Union; and now his pen is for ever still. For very many years the Committee enjoyed the benefit of Mr. W. H. G. Kingston's services, for he thoroughly appreciated their desire to provide healthy and stimulating literature for the young, even though it were not of a decidedly didactic or religious type. With this view, in 1866 *Kind Words* was projected, and it continued its career until the beginning of 1880, when it gave place to *Young England*, a weekly serial of larger dimensions, but issued with the same aim and purpose. All through these years Mr. Kingston's pen was more or less employed, and some of his best stories were issued from this office. This much is stated in justice to the author and the publishers, who for many years have fully recognised the importance of counteracting the evil influence of vicious literature, and have been doing their utmost to create a taste for sound and instructive reading.

The following story is not one of reckless adventure, nor one in which fighting and bloodshed are introduced to fan a spurious spirit of heroism. It is the reproduction of a page of history, and a most important one, when good men held not their lives dear to uphold and defend that which was dearer than life—civil and religious liberty.

The example of Blake is held up to the boys of to-day, not because he fought and conquered, but because he was a conscientious, God-fearing man, and his conscience told him that the best interests of his country demanded resistance to the Stuart rule. Such a man as Blake was a hero everywhere, and needed not a quarter-deck to display his heroism.

56, OLD BAILEY.

LIST OF ENGRAVINGS.

CONTENTS.

THE BOY
WHO SAILED WITH BLAKE.

CHAPTER I.

MY FRIENDS AND I.

"HARK! the bells of St. Michael's are sending forth a jovial peal!" exclaimed Lancelot Kerridge, as he, Dick Harvey, and I were one day on board his boat fishing for mackerel, about two miles off the sea-port town of Lyme. "What they are saying I should mightily like to know, for depend on't it's something of importance. Haul in the lines, Ben!" he continued, addressing me; "and, Dick, put an oar out to windward. I'll take the helm. We shall fetch the Cob by keeping our luff."

The wind was off shore, but as we were to the westward of the Cob, and the tide was making in the same direction, we could easily fetch it. The water was smooth, the sea blue and bright as the eyes of sweet Cicely Kerridge, my friend Lancelot's young sister, while scarcely a cloud dimmed the clear sky overhead.

Lyme, then containing but one thousand inhabitants

B

where my two companions and I lived, is situated in Dorsetshire, near its western border, on the northern shore of a wide bay, formed by the Bill of Portland on the east and the Start Point on the west. Along the coast are several other towns, of which Dartmouth, owing to its excellent harbour, is the most considerable, besides numerous villages, including Charmouth and Uplyme. A line of cliffs of no great height extends away on either side of Lyme, which stands at the bottom of a valley; while beyond it rise the green slopes of Colway and Uplyme, hills overlooking the town.

On the eastern side was the house of my father, Captain Roger Bracewell. He had commanded several of the trading ships of Master Humphry Blake, of Bridgewater, at one time a merchant of renown, and the father of Captain Robert Blake, who had already made his name famous for his gallant defence of Prior's Hill when Bristol was besieged by Prince Rupert, until it was yielded in a dastardly fashion by Governor Fiennes. My father retiring from the sea with a competency, having married late in life, settled in Lyme, his native place. His house, which overlooked the bay, was of the better sort, with curious gables, and a balcony supported on strong wooden pillars in front, where he was wont to sit, smoking his pipe, and enjoying a view of the ocean he still loved full well, with the ships—their white canvas spread to the breeze—sailing by in the distance, or approaching to take shelter in our roadstead.

There were a few other residences of the same character; but most of the houses were built of soft stone, with thatched roofs, forming four irregular narrow streets, with several narrower lanes of no very dignified character. Still, we were fond of our little town, and had reasons to be proud of it from the events I am about to describe.

My two friends and I spent much of our time on the water. Lancelot, my senior by two years, was the son of the worshipful Master Kerridge, Mayor of Lyme, and Dick's father was Mr. Harvey, a man of considerable wealth and influence in the neighbourhood, brother-in-law of Mr. Ceely, who had been made Governor of the town by the Parliament.

Our fathers were Puritans and staunch Parliamentarians. They had become so in consequence of the faithlessness of the King, and the attempt of Laud to introduce Popish rites and to enslave the consciences of free-born Englishmen. Who, indeed, could have witnessed the clipping of ears, the slitting of noses, the branding of temples, and burning of tongues, to which the Archbishop resorted to crush Nonconformity—who could have seen their friends imprisoned, placed in the pillory, and even scourged through the streets, without feeling their hearts burn with indignation and their whole souls rebel against tyranny so outrageous?

"It is a wonder that any honest man could be found to support that miscreant Laud," I remember hearing my father say. "He and his faithless master are mainly answerable for the civil strife now devastating, from north to south and east to west, our fair English land."

But I must not trouble my readers with politics; my object is to narrate the scenes I witnessed, or the events in which I took a part. I was too young, indeed, at that time to think much about the matter, but yet I was as enthusiastic a Roundhead as any of my fellow-townsmen. As we approached the little harbour we passed through a large fleet of traders, brought up in the roadstead for shelter, most of which, belonging to London merchants, dared not therefore put into any port held by the Cavaliers. Three or four had dropped their anchors while we were out fishing. We hailed one of them, which had come in from the westward, to ask the news.

"Bad news!" was the answer. "The Malignants have taken Exeter, and many other places in the west country, and are now marching in great force on London."

"I hope they won't come to Lyme on their way, for if they do, we shall have but small chance of withstanding them," I observed to my companions as we sailed on.

"I have but little fear on that score," replied Lancelot. "We'll fight while a man remains on his legs, or a gun can be fired from our batteries."

Lancelot's enthusiasm inspired me. The breeze freshened. We soon rounded the Cob, when we pulled up among the small craft which crowded the harbour, to a spot where Lancelot usually kept his boat. As soon as we had moored her we sprang on shore, and hurried through the lower part of the town, which was almost deserted.

We found the greater portion of the inhabitants collected at the northern side; and I had scarcely time to ask a question of my father, whom I joined, before we saw a body of troops approaching, led by an officer on horseback. He was a strong-built man, of moderate height, with a fair and florid complexion, and, contrary to the fashion general among Puritans, his hair, in rich profusion, was seen escaping beneath his broad-brimmed hat, while he wore large whiskers, but no beard—his countenance unmistakably exhibiting firmness and determination. He returned in a cordial manner the salutes of the principal townsmen, who had gone out to meet him.

"Who is he?" I asked of my father.

"That, my son, is Colonel Blake. He has come with five hundred men of Popham's regiment, to protect us from a large army of Malignants—twenty thousand men, it is said —under Prince Maurice, cousin to the King. He threatens to annihilate our little town; but though we shall have a hard struggle to beat them back, God will protect the right."

The bells we had heard had been set ringing on the announcement of the approach of Colonel Blake; and now, as he and his brave followers entered the town, they pealed forth with redoubled energy.

While the men were sent to their quarters, he, accompanied by the Governor and Mayor, and several officers, rode round the outskirts of the town, to point out the spots where he judged it necessary that batteries and entrenchments should be thrown up.

He was accompanied by a young nephew, also named Robert Blake, son of his brother Samuel, who was killed some time before at Bridgewater, while commanding a company in Colonel Popham's regiment. I afterwards became well acquainted with young Robert Blake, as we were much drawn together by the fondness for a sea life which we both possessed. His was rather a passion than a mere fondness—indeed, like his noble uncle, he was enthusiastic in all his aspirations, and a more gallant, noble-minded lad I never met.

That evening the newly arrived troops, as well as every man in the place capable of labouring, set to work with pickaxes, spades, and barrows to throw up embankments, to cut trenches, to erect batteries, to barricade the roads, and to loophole all the outer walls of the houses and gardens. Officers were in the meantime despatched by the Governor and the Mayor to obtain volunteers from Charmouth, Uplyme, and other villages; while foraging parties were sent out in all directions to collect provisions, cattle, and fodder. Although, in addition to Colonel Blake's five hundred regulars, scarcely more than three hundred fighting men could be mustered in the town, there were no signs of wavering; but high and low endeavoured to make amends for the paucity of their numbers by their dauntless courage, their energy, and unceasing toil; and even women and children were to be seen in all directions, filling baskets with sods, and carrying materials to the labourers at the earthworks.

Lancelot and I kept together, and did our best to be of use, though I could not do much, being a little fellow; but I know that I worked away as hard as my strength would allow me. Colonel Blake was everywhere, superintending the operations and encouraging the men. Stopping near where my friends and I were at work, he addressed the labourers.

"The haughty Cavaliers fancy that they can ride rough-shod into your little town, my lads," he said; "but I want you to show them that you can fight for your hearths and homes as well as did my brave fellows at Prior's Hill; and I do not fear that a traitor will be found within our trenches to deliver up the place, while we have a cask of powder in our magazines, or a musket to fire it. And even should our ammunition run short, the Lord of Hosts being with us, we'll drive them back with pike and sword."

"Rightly spoken, Colonel Blake," said my father, who had just then reached the spot where the Colonel was standing. "I am an old man, and had looked forward to ending my days in peace; but willingly will I promise you that the enemy shall march over my dead body before they get within our entrenchments. I served on board the ships of your honoured father, when we had many a tough fight with corsairs, Spaniards, Portingales, and Dutchmen; and I feel sure that I shall not draw my sword in vain when his son commands. Maybe you may remember Richard Bracewell?"

"Well indeed I do," answered Colonel Blake, putting out his hand and warmly shaking that of my father. "And many a long yarn about your adventures have I listened to with eager interest, while I longed to sail over the wide ocean and to visit the strange countries you described. Who is that youngster standing by you?" he then asked in a kindly tone, looking down on me.

"My only boy, the son of my old age," answered my father. "Though young now, he will, I trust, ere long grow big enough to fight for the civil and religious liberties of our country, or to defend her from foreign foes."

"Judging by his looks, and knowing whose son he is, I would gladly have him with me when he is old enough, should heaven spare our lives; but at present he is too young to be exposed to the dangers of war, and I would advise you to keep him under lock and key when the fight is going on, or he will be running where bullets and round shot are falling, and perhaps his young life will be taken before he has had time to strike a blow for the liberties of our country."

"I hope that I can do something now, sir," I said, not liking the thoughts of being shut up. "I can fire a pistol if I cannot point an arquebuse; and since morning I have carried a hundred baskets or more of earth to the embankment."

"You speak bravely, my boy, and bravely you will act when the time comes," said the Colonel, and forthwith he addressed himself to others who came to receive his orders. Such was my first introduction to one with whom I was destined to serve for many a year.

I well remember the spot where we were standing. On one side lay the blue sea extending to the horizon, below us was the town with its white-walled, straw-thatched buildings, the church with its spire to the left, and before us were the green slopes of the hills sprinkled here and there with clumps of trees, while on the more level spots were to be seen corn-fields and orchards smiling in the rays of the setting sun. Beyond the town was Colway House, a substantial mansion, once the residence of the Cobham family; and about a mile from it, on the opposite side of the valley, was a collection of buildings known as Hayes Farm, both of which had been fortified, and occupied as outposts.

We had, we knew, not many days to prepare for the defence; and I am proud to say that, scrap of a boy as I was, I worked as hard as many of my elders. Late in the evening, when it was already dusk, my father found me, with Lancelot and Dick, still at our self-imposed task.

"Come, boys," he said, "it is time for you to go home and get some sleep. You must leave it to stronger men to labour during the night."

"Just let us carry a few more basketfuls, sir," answered Lancelot. "See that gap; we have undertaken to fill it up, and, for what we can tell, the enemy may be upon us before the morning."

"Well, well, lads, I like your spirit. I will not baulk you. Give me a spade; I will try what I can do to expedite the work." And my revered father, as soon as the spade had been handed to him, began digging away with right goodwill, filling the baskets, which were carried up to the embankment. He soon became so interested in the work that he was as unwilling to knock off as we were.

"Run back and get a lantern. Its light will help us to finish our task more quickly. Maybe the host of the 'Three Tankards' will lend thee one; or Master Harris who lives opposite; or, if you cannot get one nearer, go home and bring our big lantern which hangs inside the hall door. See that it is well trimmed, though."

"Ay, ay, father," I answered, and set off. Knowing every foot of the way, I was not afraid of running, even though the gathering darkness made it difficult to see objects at any distance beyond my nose.

At the first places where I called, all the lanterns had

been put into requisition, and so I had to run on until I reached our house. I found my sister Audrey, and Margaret our maid, wondering why we were so long absent. Supper was on the table, and the viands getting cold. On hearing why I wanted the lantern, they both wished to come and help us, Audrey declaring that she could carry a basket as well as either of us boys.

"You must stop and take care of the house," I answered, feeling a little jealous that a girl should fancy she could work as well as my companions and I. "There are a good many strangers in the town, and it would not do to leave the house empty. Margaret can trim the lantern, as she knows how to do it better than I do. Be quick about it, for I must be off again as fast as my legs can carry me."

"Take a crust of bread and a piece of cheese in the meantime, Master Ben," said Margaret, as she took down the lantern, and examined the wick.

"I have no time for eating; I am not hungry," I answered, and I watched her impatiently, while she poured in some fresh oil. Taking the lantern as soon as it was lighted, I hurried out, and, holding it before me, ran on without fear of rushing against any one coming from an opposite direction. I had got a short distance when I found myself in the midst of a body of men, who were coming up from the harbour carrying loads on their shoulder. They had, I discovered from the remarks which reached me, just landed.

"Do you bring any news?" I inquired.

"Fine news, young sir," answered one of the men. "Prince Maurice has been driven away from Plymouth, which he tried to take, but couldn't. But, as maybe he will pay a visit to Lyme, we have brought you powder and shot, and other munitions of war, and no doubt Colonel Blake will make good use of them."

Having obtained all the information I could from the communicative seaman, I hurried on with the satisfactory intelligence to the works, where I found my father leaning on his spade, pretty well tired out by his unusual exertions. The light of the lantern I brought, however, enabled us to proceed, and he recommenced digging with as much energy as before.

As we were running backwards and forwards, I could see numerous other lights all along the line, within a few yards of each other, marking the spots where the people were working.

It was nearly midnight before our task was concluded. Not one of us had felt hungry or thirsty. My father then insisted on our returning home, and on our way we left Lancelot and Dick at their respective homes.

We found Audrey and Margaret sitting up for us, both looking somewhat pale, naturally supposing that if the finishing of the earthworks was so important, immediate danger was to be apprehended. Supper over, we knelt in prayer, which, on all occasions and under all circumstances, was our wont. Then retiring to bed, I for one slept like a top. Next day was like the previous one.

The news that Prince Maurice, at the head of a vast army, was marching into Dorsetshire, spread through the town and incited every one to renewed exertions. Volunteers, who came in from all sides, were being drilled by Colonel Weir and other officers, most of them having to learn not only the use of the pike and sword, but how to load and fire an arquebuse or musket.

The soldiers and townsmen were still labouring away at the fortifications, when one morning, as Lancelot, Dick, and I were employed at the top of an embankment, my father helping us, we saw a horseman who had been on outpost duty come galloping down the hill towards the town.

"The enemy are near at hand!" he exclaimed, as he rode up to where Colonel Blake and Governor Ccely stood. "They will be here anon. I could see them defiling along the road like a host of ants. I had to ride hard to escape their advance guard."

On receiving this news, the colonel ordered the drums to beat to arms. Parties were sent out to strengthen the two outposts, and the troops and townsmen, with the volunteers, hastened to the lines.

"How many fighting men have we?" I asked of my father, as I watched the defenders taking up their appointed positions.

"Colonel Blake brought five hundred men with him, and, maybe, with the townsmen and volunteers from the neighbourhood, we shall muster well-nigh another five hundred," he answered.

"A thousand men to withstand twenty thousand?" I asked in a doubtful tone.

"Each man of the one thousand will count for twenty when fighting in a just cause," he answered. "Colonel Blake thinks that we can not only withstand, but drive back the Malignants, or he would not wantonly throw away our lives."

We watched eagerly for some time, when at length horse and foot, gay banners flying, cuirasses and helmets glittering in the bright sun, appeared over the brow of the distant hills. On they came, until every height was crowned, and we saw drawn up in battle array what appeared to us an army sufficient at a single charge to overwhelm our slender defences.

There they remained. We could see horsemen galloping to and fro on the sides of the hills, but as yet not a shot had been fired.

Sentries were posted along our whole line, and the men

were ordered to sit down and take their dinners. I saw my father look graver than usual.

"Ben," he said, "I have been consulting with Master Kerridge, and he agrees with me that it would be wrong to allow you boys to expose your lives. I promise you that if you can render service to the cause you shall be employed; and you must all three give me your words that you will remain where I place you, and not come forth until you are sent for."

Very unwillingly Lancelot and Dick and I gave the promise exacted from us, though we were more content when my father took us to the church, and told us that we might remain in the tower, whence, as it overlooked the greater portion of the lines, we could see through a narrow loophole what was going forward.

He then returned to the post which he, with Martin Shobbrok, an old follower of his in many a voyage, had undertaken to keep. He had directed me, should the enemy get into the town, to run home and try to protect my sister from insult, and our house from plunder. "Though I may never return, my boy, should the Malignants force an entrance, yet you, Ben, will, I trust, live to become a man, and serve our country either on shore or afloat," he said in a grave tone, which showed, however, no signs of fear. I often afterwards thought of his words, and prayed that I might fulfil his expectations.

We had not long taken up our position in the tower before we saw the Cavalier forces moving down the slopes of the hill. One party advanced towards our outposts at Hayes Farm, and then attacked Colway House, at which their great guns commenced a furious fire, wreaths of white smoke filling the calm air. Presently the two little garrisons returned the salute with right goodwill.

Then we caught sight of them rushing at full speed

COLONEL BLAKE DEFYING THE ENEMY.

towards our lines ; and good reason they had to move fast, for, following them close, came horse and foot in battle array, with trumpets sounding, drums beating, lances in rest, pikes at the charge, and swords flashing in the bright sunlight. The enemy halted, however, when still at a distance, and a herald advanced, who blowing a blast on his trumpet summoned the town instantly to surrender.

Colonel Blake, mounting on the ramparts, answered in a loud tone, which reached our ears—

"Not while we have men to fight, or breastworks to defend the place. Go, tell the Prince who sent you that such is our resolve."

Shaking his fist at the town, the herald wheeled round his horse and galloped off.

But a short time elapsed before the trumpets sounded a general charge, and the infantry rushed impetuously forward towards the lines, hurling immense numbers of hand-grenades among the defenders, which, bursting as they fell, filled the air with smoke and deafened our ears by their explosions.

Not one of our brave fellows wavered, but fired rapidly in return among the dense masses of the foe. The next instant we could see a large body of cavalry riding furiously onward, expecting to gain an easy victory. In vain the bravest attempted to ride over the earthworks, up to the very muzzles of the muskets ; but they were driven back by the heavy fire poured into their ranks, and compelled to retreat up the valley, leaving many dead and wounded behind.

We three boys could not refrain from giving way to a shout of joy, believing that the battle was won; but we were grievously mistaken. Again the serried ranks of foot advanced with fierce shouts, threatening the destruction of our little garrison.

CHAPTER II.

A SUCCESSFUL DISGUISE.

N came the enemy with determination. Fiercely the battle raged—again and again the foot advanced up to the embankment, each time retreating from the storm of bullets, case shot, and round shot poured into them, leaving the ground strewed with their comrades, some in the calm of death, others struggling in vain efforts to rise and escape from the field.

Again we thought that the fight for that day was over, when we distinguished a horseman riding along the broken ranks of the Cavaliers, waving his sword, as if to lead them on. He advanced, but not a foot would they budge. They had that day gained a lesson they could not so easily forget.

At length, losing patience, the Cavalier, who we had no doubt was the Prince himself, rode round to where his cavalry were posted. The advance was sounded, and now the horse, drawn up in the rear, urged forward the foot with lances and pistol shots at their backs.

"They must come on this time," cried Lancelot; "if they don't, they'll get cut down by their friends in the rear."

"Then I hope that such will be their fate," said Dick. "See, the poor fellows are advancing. I pity them, for they well know how they will be treated by Colonel Blake."

As the enemy got within range of our firearms they were received with showers of musket balls and case shot, which went through and through their closed ranks, striking down dozens at a time, but still, urged on by their officers—who, to give them their due, fought with the most heroic bravery—they advanced close up to our lines. Here they were met by pistols, pikes, and spears, and then, staggering, they broke and fled, followed by showers of missiles, until they were beyond our reach.

A loud shout rose all along our line, in which we in the tower joined right heartily, but our troops were too wearied with the ceaseless exertions they had made during the whole of the afternoon to pursue the fugitives; indeed, it would have been the very thing the Prince would have desired, as he would have been down upon them with his cavalry, and although they might have retreated to the lines, many a valuable life would have been sacrificed, and no advantage gained.

Colonel Blake therefore contented himself with the brilliant success he had achieved. He had shown those haughty Cavaliers that the garrison of Lyme was not to be so easily overcome as they had thought, and had taught them what they were to expect should they again venture to assail us.

Such was the termination of the first day of the siege. Descending from our tower with the satisfaction of having faithfully fulfilled our promise, we went down the lines to view more nearly the battle-field. The whole ground was strewed near and far off with the bodies of men and horses. Parties were at once sent out to bring in any who might be still living, and to bury the dead while the rays

c

of the setting sun gleamed on the white tents of the Royalist camp, which could be seen in the distance.

Few doubted that another day would see a fresh attack made on our entrenchments, but some were sanguine enough to believe that the Prince, after the lesson he had received, would retire. I asked my father what he thought. He answered—

"The Royalists will not go away without further attempts to reduce the town, for they know too well that if they do they will leave a vigilant enemy in their rear, under whose standard thousands of honest Puritans will gladly gather to destroy the enemies of our country's freedom."

The next morning it was seen that the Cavaliers were busy erecting batteries and throwing up earthworks on all the neighbouring heights, so that they might command our forts and batter down our houses.

Notwithstanding the preparations made for the destruction of the town, Colonel Blake urged the garrison to resist to the bitter end, assuring them that ere that should come Parliament would send them relief.

I cannot attempt to give a detailed account of the siege. Soon after his first repulse, Prince Maurice opened fire from his great guns placed on all the heights commanding the town, from the effects of which not only the houses but our forts suffered. In a short time the fort at the Cob was knocked to pieces by a battery which had been thrown up at Holme Bush, which also swept the bay, so as to render it dangerous for any vessel to enter the harbour in the day time. Information was also received that the Cavaliers were busy throwing up another battery at Colway Hill, in front of Colway House, and into this battery they were seen dragging some of their largest ordnance. As it commanded Davies Fort, which was the key of our defences, the Colonel ordered a large body of men to strengthen that fort as rapidly as possible. Volunteers were not lacking, and Lancelot and I were allowed to help. We called for Dick Harvey on the way, and when the men saw three young gentlemen, the sons of the three principal persons in the place, labouring away as hard as any one, it encouraged them to still greater exertions, and in a few hours a bank twelve feet thick had been thrown up, which it was not likely the shot from the enemy's guns could penetrate. Colonel Blake passing while we were thus occupied, patted me on the head.

" Well done, young comrade," he said in a kind tone. " If we had a garrison of a few hundred boys like you, we might hold the place against all assailants, without the help of more veteran troops."

The earthworks had been completed, and Lancelot and I were standing on the top, surveying with no little pride the portion we had assisted in throwing up, when I saw a puff of smoke issue from Colway Hill, followed by a thundering report, and a round shot plunged into the bank close beneath our feet.

" Come down, youngsters ! " shouted my father, who had just before entered the fort. " More of those iron balls will be coming in this direction. You must not run the risk of losing your lives when you cannot advance our good cause."

We unwillingly obeyed, but we had not gone far before a succession of reports showed that the enemy had already got several guns into position, and had not the fort been strengthened, it would soon have been rendered untenable. Numerous successive attacks were made, but were repulsed as the first had been.

Poor little Audrey and Cicely were in a great state of alarm while the firing continued, naturally fearing that the whole town would soon be battered down.

At length, however, the Royalists drew off, and we were left in quiet for nearly a week. The time was spent in strengthening the fortifications and drilling the volunteers. We had spies in the camp of the Cavaliers, who managed under cover of the night to come into the town with information of what they were about. One piece of news they brought caused Governor Ceely and my friend Dick much anxiety. It was that Mr. Harvey, Dick's father, who, having been absent from the town when the Cavalier army arrived before it, had been unable to join us, was made prisoner, and was now in the camp. Dick was afraid that the Prince would hang him, as he had others, and talked much with Lancelot and me of a plan for rescuing him ; still, for a long time we could strike out nothing feasible. Dick, like a good son, was ready to run every risk, and I was ready to assist him if I could obtain my father's leave, as was also Lancelot.

We took Audrey and Cicely into our councils. Audrey proposed that she and Cicely should go to the camp and try to bribe the guards to let Mr. Harvey escape.

"Bad as the Cavaliers may be, they won't injure two young girls, and Prince Maurice, who is a gentleman, would be sure to treat us with courtesy," observed Audrey. "You, Lancelot, and Dick might, in the meantime, during the night, row along the coast, and landing, obtain a horse, with which you can wait outside the Royalists' camp, until Mr. Harvey, being free, finds you and gallops off."

"No, no, such a plan I can never agree to," exclaimed Lancelot. "I would sooner trust you two girls in a den of lions than amongst those Malignants. We must devise some other plan; I am sure that our fathers would not consent. Mr. Harvey was taken without arms, and nothing can be proved against him."

This conversation took place on the 6th of May, 1644, and good reason I had for remembering the date. The weather had hitherto been fine, but soon after midday it began to blow hard from the southward, and the seas came rolling into our little harbour. Lancelot, who had gone away, returned in a hurry, accompanied by Dick, and asked him to assist in hauling up his boat, which ran a chance of being dashed to pieces, as Tom Noakes, who had charge of her, was likely to be engaged on the lines. We all three hurried down. When we got there, we found a number of men, who, as the enemy were quiet, had left their posts in order to secure their craft from the tempest. Evening was approaching, and as the gale was rapidly increasing there was no time to be lost. We found the boat tumbling and tossing about at her moorings, exposed to great risk of being run down by the smaller vessels which were standing in for shelter. To get on board was the difficulty, as no other boat was at hand, so Lancelot, pulling off his clothes, and swimming through the foaming sea, was soon on board.

"Stand by, to haul her up as she comes in," he shouted out, as he cast off the moorings. Then springing aft, he seized an oar. It was well that he did so, for just then a vessel which had rounded the Cob came tearing up under her foresail, the man at the helm apparently not seeing the boat in the way.

Lancelot shouted lustily and plied his oar, the craft just scraping the stern of the boat as she luffed up to come to an anchor. We were on the east shore, the most exposed side of the harbour, it should be understood. Dick and I stood by to seize the boat as she struck the beach. Lancelot, leaping on shore, slipped into his shirt and hauled away likewise, but with our united strength we could scarcely have succeeded, had not Martin Shobbrok come to our aid. Fortunately there were some rollers near at hand, and by their means we at length got the boat hauled up out of harm's way.

Never had I seen our harbour in a state of greater confusion. The smaller craft continued to stand in sometimes two or three together, many of them running foul of one another before they could bring up, and others being driven on shore.

The larger vessels outside were getting down fresh anchors, and several making sail were endeavouring to beat out of the bay, to obtain an offing where they could ride out the gale.

A large number of the townsmen were engaged in securing the vessels, when sounding high above the roar of the tempest a rapid fusilade was heard in the direction of the lines, while shot after shot from the enemy's batteries came hurtling into the town.

"The soldiers would be at their suppers at this hour," exclaimed Martin. "I fear me much that the place has been surprised, and if so, it will go hard with us. Hasten to your homes, young gentlemen, and await the issue; I must to my post."

Martin, without waiting to see what we should do, taking his musket, which he had placed near the boat, hurried away, as did all the men engaged in securing the vessels. We followed, eager to know what was taking place. The sound of bursting hand-grenades, the reports of muskets and pistols, the shouts and shrieks which reached our ears, showed us that the fight was raging much nearer than usual.

"There's no doubt about the enemy being in the town," cried Lancelot. "We may as well die fighting as be killed like rats in a hole. Come on, lads!"

We dashed forward through the market square, in a street leading from which towards the lines we could see, by the bright and rapid flashes, that hot fighting was going on. A party from the harbour had come up just in time to stop the entrance into the square, and with loud shouts they pressed onwards, while from the windows of every house there burst forth bright flashes from arquebuse, musket, and pistol. To force our way in that direction was impossible, so, led by Lancelot, we made a wide circuit, until we reached the neighbourhood of the lines, where we found a furious fight was also raging.

We met on our way several wounded men supported by mourning parties of women, who had ventured up, even to the scene of the conflict, for the sake of succouring those who had been struck down. Still, the fight in the centre of the town continued, and at length we learned from one of the wounded men that a large body of Cavaliers had forced their way into the town, when Colonel Blake, closing in on their rear, had cut them off, but though Malignants as they were, like gallant men they were fighting desperately.

Meanwhile another party outside were endeavouring to drive back the garrison and rescue them. The darkness increased, the south wind bringing up a thick fog, which prevented our assailants from seeing their way. Often the hand-grenades they intended for us were thrown among their own companions, while our people plied them with every weapon which could be mustered. The bullets came pinging against the wall above where we were standing, but in our eagerness we boys heeded not the risk we were running.

"Let us fight too!" exclaimed Lancelot, and we made our way on to the trenches, where not only the soldiers, the volunteers, and the townsmen were fighting, but women, with muskets in their hands, were firing away, encouraging their companions with shouts and cheers. Lancelot had got hold of a musket belonging to one of the garrison who had fallen, and had taken his powder-horn and shot-belt. Dick and I, after hunting about, succeeded in finding a couple of horse-pistols, but scarcely had we

fired them than the din in front of us ceased, though the
report of firearms to the right and left of us still continued.
We could hear the tramp of men and the cries and groans
of the wounded in front, but the uproar towards the
market-place was quelled. No shots were heard, no clashing of swords, no shouts and shrieks.

"The enemy have retreated! The Malignants are flying!" was the cry passed along the lines.

Still, we could scarcely believe it possible. But an hour
had passed since the attack had commenced, and our little
garrison had driven back once more the well-equipped
troops of Prince Maurice.

The storm raged fiercely during the night, and many
fearing that another attack might be made, the greater
portion of the garrison remained under arms, ready for
any emergency.

Not until morning was the full extent of the Cavaliers'
loss discovered. Within the lines well-nigh four hundred
men lay stark and stiff where they had fallen, struck down
by the fire from the houses and the fierce onslaught in
front and rear, few prisoners having been taken.

Outside the trenches a hundred more strewed the ground,
among them many officers of distinction, including Colonel
Blewett, a gallant gentleman, greatly esteemed by Maurice.
We knew this, because early in the morning the Prince
sent a herald to request that he might be restored if a prisoner, or that his body might be given up if dead.

A prisoner he was not, for every officer who had come
inside the lines had been slain. The Colonel answered that
the body should be restored if found, provided our people
were not injured while searching for it and burying the
dead. Before long the body of the Cavalier was discovered
where he had fallen, at the entrance of the town, leading
on his men. It was placed with all decency in a coffin, and

Colonel Blake sent word that it was ready to be delivered up, and that he hoped, in return, his friend Mr. Harvey would be set at liberty.

The Prince, to the indignation of the garrison, replied that they might keep the body, and refused to give up Mr. Harvey. The coffin was, notwithstanding, carried to the lines opposite Holme Bush, when a signal was made to the heralds to come for it. Colonel Blake stood by to receive them.

" Have you any orders to pay for the shroud and coffin ? " he asked.

" We have received none," was the answer.

" Take them, notwithstanding," answered the Colonel, curling his whiskers, as was his wont when angered. " We are not so poor but that we can afford to give them to you."

The body was taken up by the men sent to fetch it, and slowly they wended their way back to the camp. An officer approached while the flag of truce was flying. He was one with whom Colonel Blake was acquainted.

" Here, friend," he said, " you see the weakness of our works. We trust not to them. Tell Prince Maurice that should he desire to come in, we will pull down a dozen yards, so that he may enter with ten men abreast, and we will give him battle."

" Not so," answered the Royalist, stung by the reproach to the military prowess of his party. " We will take our own time, but will come ere long."

The Colonel replied by a scornful laugh.

All that day we enjoyed unusual quiet, for the Royalists had not the heart again to attack us, though we were well aware they would do so should occasion favour them.

Day after day and week after week went by, still our garrison held out. Our provisions were running short, as was our ammunition, and should that fail us—notwithstanding all the heroic efforts which had been made—we should be compelled to yield.

My friend Dick was still very anxious about his father.

"I have an idea!" exclaimed Lancelot. "You, Dick, are like your sister Mildred. Probably the Prince is not aware she is not in the town. What say you to dressing up in her clothes, and taking Ben with you? he can pretend to be your brother. He looks so young, no one would think of injuring him more than they would you, supposing you to be a girl. You can steal out at night; go boldly to the Prince, and say you wish to see your father. He will scarcely refuse you. You can then tell Mr. Harvey your plan, and he is a man of wealth; the chances are he'll find the means of bribing his guards. I meantime will sail along the shore, and landing, arrange as I proposed about a horse, which I will have ready at the foot of Charmouth Rise."

We kept our plan secret. I had some doubt whether I was acting rightly, but I trusted that my father would not blame me. Audrey and Cicely were delighted, and soon rigged up Dick, so that the keenest eye would not have discovered that he was a boy.

That very night Lancelot, accompanied by Tom Noakes, who had charge of his boat, put out of the harbour, and favoured by a light breeze, stood along the shore. We slipped out and crept along past the sentries, making our way to the east of Colway Hill. Every moment we expected to be discovered, but a thick fog favoured our design, and we got away, creeping along hedges and under banks, until we were clear outside the enemy's entrenchments as well as our own.

Proceeding northward, we reached a wide-spreading tree on the top of a high bank, where we sat down to rest and consult as to our future course. The moon rising and the fog blowing off, we saw spread out before us the white

" WHO ARE YOU, MY PRETTY MAIDEN ? "

tents of the Cavalier army, covering a wide extent of ground. We agreed that it would be wise to wait until daylight, lest, approaching the camp, we might be shot by the sentries. Dick produced some food which he had brought in his pocket. We ate it with good appetites. We then stretched ourselves on the sward, not supposing that we should go to sleep, but in spite of our anxiety we dropped off. When we awoke it was broad daylight.

It was fortunate we were not discovered, for Dick's dress looked so draggled and dirty that no one would have taken him for a young lady. I set to work to brush and clean him, and make him more presentable. We had resolved to walk boldly on unless challenged, until we could reach the Prince's tent, when Dick would ask leave as if his request was sure to be granted to see his father as though on family matters. If refused, we would wait about the camp until we could find an opportunity of gaining our object. We came sooner than we expected on a sentry, who at once challenged us.

"You won't stop us, my good man," answered Dick, going up and slipping a silver crown into his hand. "We have come to see our father, and surely you would not interfere with two young children like us, who can do no harm to anyone."

The man, a fresh recruit, who knew nothing about military discipline, having pocketed the coin, was easily persuaded to allow us to proceed. The next sentry Dick managed in the same way. We advanced, Dick holding my hand, until we were within the camp. Several persons spoke to us, but did not seem to think it necessary to interfere with our progress, and at length, by dint of inquiring the way, we found ourselves standing before a large tent, occupied, we were told, by Prince Maurice.

We were waiting for leave to enter, when the curtain

was drawn aside, and a Cavalier in cuirass and plumed hat, a light moustache, his locks curling over his shoulders, came forth.

"Who are you, my pretty maiden ?" he asked, looking at Dick.

"An' it please you, sir, I've come to see my father, who, we have heard, is a prisoner in the camp, though why or wherefore he is detained we cannot tell, for no more peaceable gentleman is to be found in the south of England. We wish to deliver some messages to him, and learn how he fares. Have we your permission, for you are, I opine, the general of this army ? "

The Prince, for that such he was we knew by the way the officers who stood round addressed him, smiled as he replied—

"Say, who is your father ? "

"Master Harvey, your highness," answered Dick.

"You have an arrant rebel for a father, then, I fear," said the Prince.

"Please, your highness, I know nothing of politics ; all I desire is to have a few words with my father, whom I am bound to honour, whether Royalist or Roundhead, and then to quit the camp and return home."

The Prince, after exchanging a few words with one of the gentlemen standing by, handed a piece of paper, on which he had written a few lines, to Dick.

"Take this, maiden," he said; " it will gain your object. But, understand, after you have seen your father, for your own sake, without loss of time, you must return home."

Thankful that we had so easily accomplished the first part of our enterprise—accompanied by one of the officers, who undertook to show us the way—we set off for the cottage in which we were told Mr. Harvey with other prisoners were confined.

CHAPTER III.

R. HARVEY looked so astonished when Dick and I were introduced, that he almost betrayed us. Quickly, however, recovering himself, he opened his arms and embraced us affectionately. The other prisoners, gentlemen well acquainted with him, seeing that he wished to be alone, retired to the farther end of the room, when Dick lost no time in whispering into his ear the plan we had arranged for his liberation.

He listened with a thoughtful brow, and Dick continued to press its adoption, but I much feared that he would not agree.

"I will try it," he said at last; "but you, my children, must hasten from the camp; it is no place for young persons, and should I fail to escape, you will be made to suffer."

Though Dick begged hard to remain, his father was firm, and told us to return by the way we had come, hoping that we might get free without further questions being asked us.

Having taken an affectionate farewell of Mr. Harvey, we set out, Dick cleverly replying to all the questions put to us, and, with much less difficulty than we had expected, we gained the outskirts of the camp. Instead of returning to Lyme, we kept on towards Charmouth, to a spot where we had agreed to meet Lancelot. To our infinite satisfaction we found that he had obtained a horse and left it in Charmouth Wood as arranged, under charge of a lad, who had been directed to stay there until Mr. Harvey appeared, being supplied with food for himself and corn for the animal.

We would gladly have remained to see the success of our undertaking, but Lancelot was impatient to get back to relieve the anxiety which his father and mother would feel when his absence was discovered. We therefore set off to return to the shore, keeping a look-out to ascertain that we were not watched.

We had reached the top of the cliffs, and were about to descend, when we caught sight in the distance of a party of horse galloping towards us.

"They are out on a foraging expedition, probably," observed Lancelot. "We must get away before they come here, or they will be apt to inquire our business."

Whether we had been seen or not, it was impossible to say. We, however, made the best of our way down the cliff; on reaching the bottom we found Tom waiting for us, and forthwith set to work to launch the boat. We had scarcely got her into the water when some of the men we had before seen appeared at the top of the cliffs. They hailed us, and ordered us to come back.

"Very likely," said Lancelot. "Shove away, Tom. Let them halloo as long as they like."

We had got out the oars, and the boat was soon in deep water. Dick took the helm while the rest of us rowed, as there was not wind enough to fill the sail had we hoisted it.

A voice from the top of the cliff again ordered us to come

back, and presently several shots pattered into the water close alongside.

"Cowards!" exclaimed Lancelot. "Even though they fancy they see a girl steering, they make no scruple of trying to hit us." The shot only made us pull the harder. Presently we saw some of the men descending the cliff, and making towards a boat which lay hauled up on the beach at some distance.

"They suspect something, and intend to pursue us," observed Lancelot. "Nevertheless, we have a good start of them, and when we get farther out, we shall feel the breeze and be able to make sail."

"And maybe the other boat hasn't any oars in her, and if so we can laugh at them," said Tom.

Lancelot told Dick to steer right out to sea. "They won't be inclined to follow us far away from the land," he observed; "and if we make for Lyme, they will guess where we come from."

We saw the men reach the boat, and presently they began to launch her. By this time we had got well beyond the range of their firearms.

"Hurrah!" cried Dick, who had been looking to the eastward. "I see a sail coming up from Portland. She's more likely to be a friend than an enemy, and if we can get on board her we may defy our pursuers."

This announcement encouraged us. We had need, however, to exert ourselves, for the soldiers had almost launched the boat, which showed us that they had found oars, or they would not have taken the trouble of putting her into the water. We could only just see what they were about, but we made out that four or five fellows had got into her.

Directly afterwards, her head being turned towards us, they gave way. Though the boat was heavy, four stout

D

hands were more than a match for us, for though Tom pulled a strong oar, Lancelot and I were scarcely equal in strength to one man.

Dick kept looking eastward. Again he cried out, "There's another sail, and another; a whole fleet of them!"

"If they are Parliament ships, they'll soon make the fellows in the boat astern put about," exclaimed Tom; but we were pulling too hard to turn our heads even for a moment. Our pursuers still kept on, but they were not near enough to allow them to fire with any chance of hitting us.

They had undoubtedly seen the ships, and thought we were going out to carry them information. This probably made them more anxious to catch us. At length the breeze, as we expected it would, freshened.

"I'll step the mast; you, Master Lancelot, go to the helm. Stand by to hoist the sail, Master Ben," cried Tom; and in half a minute we had the mast stepped, the sail hoisted, and the sheet hauled aft, when, again getting out the oars, we glided rapidly through the water. We saw that our pursuers had no sail, or they would have hoisted it. This was satisfactory, though they were pulling harder than ever.

Should the wind hold, we had good hope that they would soon be left behind, still it would be folly to relax our efforts.

"Hurrah! we are distancing them," cried Tom.

As he spoke, our pursuers fired two shots at us, but the bullets fell into the water astern.

"Blaze away as fast as you like!" cried Lancelot; "every shot you fire will help us to get ahead of you."

The men in the boat had to throw in their oars to fire, while they lost some time in reloading.

The ships were still a long way off, and it was very probable that, as evening came on, the wind would fail before we could reach them. There was, however, one frigate ahead, which, propelled by oars as well as sails, was making good way. We steered for her.

"All right, boys," cried Tom; "I see the Parliamentary flag flying from her peak, and if those fellows come near us they'll have to rue it."

Notwithstanding, our pursuers, finding that they could not reach us with their muskets, again took to their oars and pulled away with might and main, trusting probably to the chances of the wind falling. Still, as we were already well ahead, we determined to maintain our advantage. The frigate meantime was coming on at good speed, carrying every stitch of canvas she could set. At length both we and the boat in chase were seen, but should the frigate fire at the latter, we might run a chance of being hit. We kept on therefore. As we got nearer, Tom stood up and waved as a signal that we wished to get on board.

On perceiving this, our pursuers knew that their game was up, and, to our regret, putting about, pulled away towards the shore as fast as they had come. The frigate, to allow us to get on board, now clewed up her sails and drew in her sweeps.

We were welcomed on board by her commander, who inquired where we had come from and what we had been about. We frankly told him, when, to our joy, he informed us that the fleet was that of the Earl of Warwick, sent by the Parliament to the relief of Lyme.

"You have come opportunely, sir," said Lancelot, "for we lack both ammunition, food, and clothing, and had you not arrived, we might in a short time have been compelled to yield to the foe."

The *Mermaid*, the frigate we had so fortunately reached, again making sail, continued her course towards Lyme. Darkness, however, quickly came on, but Tom piloted her up to a berth close in with the harbour, where none of the enemy's shot could reach her. We then accompanied Captain Ray, her commander, on shore, to convey the joyful intelligence of the approach of the Earl of Warwick's fleet.

The news spread through the town quickly, but Colonel Blake issued orders that no demonstration should be made. My father, when he had heard of our expedition, did not blame me for having taken part in it.

" Ben," he said, " you should have trusted me; and, my boy, let me urge you never to undertake anything for which you cannot ask the blessing of your Father in heaven as well as your earthly parent. Now go to rest. Before to-morrow evening important events may have occurred."

On rising the next morning, I saw a goodly array of ships at anchor before the town. Soon after I had left home I met my friend Lancelot, and we hurried down to have a look at them.

While standing on the quay, Colonel Blake with two other officers came down, about to embark to hold a consultation with the Earl.

" Would you like to accompany us and see the big ships ?" he asked, looking kindly at Lancelot and me.

We doffed our hats, and answered that it was the very thing we wished.

" Come, then !" he said; and we followed him and his companions into the boat. We pulled away for the *Vanguard*, one of the largest ships, on the deck of which the Earl stood ready to receive Colonel Blake.

Briefly exchanging greetings, they went to work on

business at once, while Lancelot and I were allowed to go round the ship to see the big guns, the huge lanterns, the stores of pikes, and the tops high up the lofty masts, each capable of holding a score of men.

"Have you a mind to sail with us, youngsters?" asked one of the officers. "You are likely boys, and will become prime seamen in time."

I answered that it was the desire of my heart, but that I must be guided by my father's wishes, for that he, being himself a master mariner, well knew the nature of the calling. The officer laughed at my reply, and I was about to ask him why he laughed, when Lancelot and I were summoned to return with Colonel Blake to the shore.

From the conversation I overheard I found that the Earl had brought, by order of Parliament, some provisions and military stores, of which we stood greatly in need. Indeed, by this time we wanted nearly everything. One-third of our men had no shoes or stockings, and large numbers were but scantily clothed, while famine had made the faces of the stoutest look pale and thin.

So shocked were the brave seamen with the appearance of the garrison, that they made collections of food and clothing on board their ships, while they gave a fourth of their daily allowance of bread for a month to supply our wants. Colonel Blake had also arranged with the Earl a plan by which it was hoped the Prince would be more signally defeated than before, should he again attack the town.

Scarcely, however, had we landed, and before the plan could be carried out, than the Cavaliers in great force once more approached our lines to attempt taking the town by assault; but Colonel Blake, hurrying to the front, placed himself at the head of a chosen band, and sallying forth drove them back. The battle lasted little more than an hour, and during that time Colonel Weir was killed, as were many other officers, and Colonel Blake himself was wounded badly in the foot, while many Cavaliers, several of them of note, lost their lives.

The next day, while the funeral of Colonel Weir was taking place, another equally sanguinary attack was made with the same result.

That night, according to a plan before arranged, three hundred seamen came on shore, and were concealed in the houses. In the morning the fleet was seen under weigh, standing towards Charmouth, now approaching the shore as if about to land some men, now firing at the Cavaliers who appeared on the cliffs.

This made the Prince fancy that part of the garrison had gone away in order to land and attack him in the rear, and that the town was even less prepared for resistance than before.

It was still early in the evening when we saw the Cavaliers in three solid columns approaching, and at the same time the big guns opened fire upon us with redoubled fury. Instead of being diminished, our little garrison had been increased by the seamen landed from the ships, so that we now mustered twelve hundred men.

As the enemy approached, the whole of our force springing into view, opened so withering a fire, that the front ranks of the foe fell into confusion. The next column coming on was treated in the same manner as the first. The big guns meanwhile battered at our earthworks, knocking down walls, and sent their shot through the roofs of the houses, many of which being set on fire were blazing up brightly.

The second column driven back as the first had been, the last advanced shouting fiercely, hoping to retrieve the day, but our brave commander was prepared for them. While he pressed them in front, his best officers appeared on their

flanks, and the seamen rushing forward leaped on them
furiously with their hangers.

In vain the gentlemen Cavaliers urged on their men.
Beaten back at every point, the soldiers took to flight, and
at length, when that summer's day closed, five hundred
Cavalier corpses strewed the ground in front of the lines.

In wanton rage at his defeat, Prince Maurice fired red-
hot balls and bars of twisted lead into the town; but no
farther attempt was made to capture it, and the following
day his army was in full retreat, he having heard that the
Earl of Essex with a large force was marching to the westward. Altogether upwards of two thousand Cavaliers lost
their lives in front of our earthworks.

To us that last day was the saddest of all. By our father's
desire, Audrey and Margaret had taken up their abode in
the house of Mr. Kerridge, as our own was greatly exposed.
Lancelot and I had been endeavouring to ascertain what
was taking place, when he saw bright flames ascending
from the direction of my father's house.

We hastened toward it. Our worst fears were realised.
Already every part was burning, while red-hot shot and
cannon balls kept ever and anon plunging into the midst of
it, preventing the possibility of extinguishing the flames.
So dangerous was the position, that Lancelot dragged me
away, and accompanied me in search of my father, to whom
I wished to give the intelligence.

As the firing in front had ceased, we went on, hoping
every now and then to meet him. It was by this time getting so dusk that we could hardly distinguish one person
from another. As we approached the part of the lines where
my father was generally posted, we met a person hurrying
towards us. He was Martin Shobbrok.

"Alack, alack! young gentlemen, I have bad news to
give you," he said. "I am hastening for a stretcher on

which to carry the captain home, though I fear much it will
be but his lifeless body."

"Where is he?" I asked, in an agony of sorrow. "Take
me to him."

"I remained with him where he fell till a surgeon came
to bind up his wounds, but from what he said I fear the
worst," answered Martin.

Hurrying on, I soon reached the spot where my dear
father lay, as Martin had told us, attended by a
surgeon.

He knew my voice, but his eyes were already growing
dim. Pressing my hand, he whispered—

"Ben, I am about to be taken from you, but I have
fallen in a righteous cause ; may you never fight for another.
And remember, my boy, do your duty in the sight of God,
and never fear what your fellow man may say or do to
you."

"I will, father," I answered, bursting into tears. "Is
there no hope?" I asked, finding that my father did not
again speak. The surgeon shook his head. Ere many
minutes had passed, my kind, brave father breathed his last.

"Poor dear Audrey will break her heart," I cried, while
Lancelot raised me from the ground.

We followed the litter on which some men, who had been
sent to collect the dead, had placed my father's body. He
received a soldier's funeral, with several other brave men
who had fallen on that day, so glorious to the national
cause.

We were orphans, but not friendless, for Mr. Kerridge
invited Audrey and me, with Margaret, to take up our
abode at his house until arrangements were made for our
future disposal. Dick had all this time received no news
of his father, and he, as were all who valued Mr. Harvey,
was in great anxiety as to his fate. Had he been unable to

make his escape, Prince Maurice would not have scrupled
to hang him, as he had other Roundheads who had fallen
into his power, when he found himself defeated.

Dick, Lancelot, and I were going along the lines picking
up bullets and searching for arms and any valuables which
might have been left by the Cavaliers, when we saw a
horseman spurring at full speed towards the town. Dick
gazed eagerly at him.

"That's my father!" he exclaimed. "I know his way
of riding. Heaven be praised!"

Dick was right. In a short time Mr. Harvey, having
thrown himself from his horse, was embracing his son.
Owing to the arrangments we had made, he had effected
his escape, though he had nearly been caught afterwards
by Prince Maurice's troops as they advanced eastward. He
came to inform Colonel Blake of the road they were taking,
and of their probable plans for the future. He brought
also news of the near approach of the Parliamentary army
under the Earl of Essex and of the recapture of
Weymouth.

The result of this information was that Colonel Blake
marched out of Lyme with his now veteran troops, and,
joined by other Roundhead forces, captured Taunton without a blow. His heroic defence of that town, when it
was soon afterwards surrounded by the Cavaliers, I cannot
describe. For a year the brave garrison held out against
all the assaults of some of the bravest of the Cavalier
leaders, including Lord Goring and his ruffian crew.

Although their clothes were reduced to rags, their
ammunition had run short, and they were almost starved,
they maintained it until relieved by General Fairfax.

In the meantime Lyme was unmolested, and Audrey and
I continued to reside with our kind friend Mr. Kerridge
and his family. A young minister undertook to super-

intend our studies, but all my leisure time was spent with Lancelot and Dick, as had been our wont before the siege, on the water.

Sometimes we extended our excursions westward as far as the Teign, and even to Dartmouth, at other times along the coast to the west of Portland Bill, but as there were no safe harbours to run to, we seldom ventured in that direction.

Colonel Blake, we heard, remained Governor of Taunton, and I much feared that I should never see him more, as he was not likely again to come to Lyme.

The battle of Naseby had been fought, and the Parliament had gained the upper hand through the length and breadth of England and Scotland, though the Royalists still held Jersey and Guernsey and Scilly, and the greater part of Ireland.

News now reached us but rarely; indeed, our little town, which had lately been so famous, seemed almost forgotten. Audrey and I, having recovered from the grief caused by the loss of our father, were very happy in our new home.

Mr. Kerridge and Mr. Harvey had arranged our affairs, so that we were not dependent upon others. At the same time it was necessary that I should have a profession. My inclinations prompted me to follow that of my father, but my friends found it difficult to settle with whom I should be sent to sea. Both Lancelot and Dick declared that they would go with me, though their fathers were not very willing that they should engage in so dangerous a calling. One day, the weather being fine, Lancelot proposed that we should make a trip to Dartmouth, taking Martin Shobbrok, now our constant companion, with us. Storing our boat with provisions for the voyage, we made sail.

We had a fine run to that beautiful little harbour, and having gone on shore, we spent more time than we had intended in purchasing various articles which were not to be procured at Lyme.

It was somewhat late in **the evening** when we stood out again, but **as** there was a moon we expected no difficulty in finding our way back; scarcely, however, had we got well **out of** the harbour than the wind shifted to the eastward, **but as** the tide was in **our favour we agreed** that by making a long leg to the southward we should fetch Lyme on the next tack.

To our disappointment, just as **we were** going about, the wind veered three points to the northward, and **we** found **it** blowing directly in our teeth. Unwilling to be defeated, we continued standing **out** to sea, expecting that when **we** went about we should **be almost** abreast of Lyme. In a short time, however, the sky became covered with thick clouds, the wind came in fitful **gusts, and** the hitherto calm ocean was broken into foam-covered **waves.**

We reduced our **sail as much as possible,** and Martin, as the most experienced, **took the helm. The night** became darker and darker. **We had no compass,** and no land could be seen. Still, supposing **that** the wind was now remaining steady, we stood on, our stout boat riding buoyantly over the increasing seas. Martin at length expressed his fear that the wind had gone back to its old quarter, and judging by the heavy foam-crested **seas** which came rolling on, that **we** were no longer under shelter of the land.

We kept up our spirits, though I guessed by the tone of Martin's voice that he **was far** from happy at our position. The tide, too, **we knew by** this time must have turned, and we should be unable to fetch **Lyme.**

We might, **we** agreed, run **back to** Dartmouth, but the attempt to find the entrance of the harbour in the darkness of the night would be difficult, if not dangerous.

Though Martin steered as well as the best of seamen, the

rising seas came washing over our bows, and we all had to
turn to and bale out the boat. This prevented us from
thinking of the danger we were in.

At length, not without risk, putting an oar out, we got
the boat round, and stood, as we supposed, towards the
shore. By this time we were wet through to the skin, and
in spite of our exertions our teeth were chattering with
cold.

"I hope Mistress Margaret will have some bowls of hot
porridge ready for us when we get in," said Lancelot.

"Oh, don't talk of that," observed Dick. "Let us get
in first. Shall we ever reach the shore, Martin, do you
think?"

"That's as God wills, Master Dick," answered Martin.
"It's our business to do our best."

Just then a sudden blast almost laid the boat over.
Martin saved her by luffing up. Scarcely had he done so
than we saw a dark object away on the starboard hand.

"That's a ship; she's standing directly down upon us,"
cried Martin. "Shout, lads, shout at the tops of your
voices."

We all shrieked out, joining Martin's deep bass, which
rose above the howling of the storm. The next instant
there came a crash, our boat had been run down, but before
she sank, having been happily struck by the bow, and not
by the stern of the ship, we found ourselves alongside,
when Martin, seizing me by the arm and catching hold of
the fore-chains, hauled me up as the boat disappeared beneath our feet. We hung there for a few seconds before
we were discovered, though I caught sight of several figures
leaning over the side. I uttered a cry of sorrow as I thought
that my two friends were lost. In vain I looked down for
them. The next instant several willing hands assisted
Martin and me on board.

" Oh, save Dick and Lancelot," I cried out. " Lower a boat ; pick them up ; don't let them perish."

My heart bounded with joy when I heard Lancelot's voice.

" Here I am, safe and sound," he cried out, running forward and shaking me by the hand, " thanks to our friends here, who hove me a rope just as I was sinking."

" And Dick, where is Dick ? " I said.

" The youngster is on board, but he got a knock on the head. He's coming round though," said a voice from the afterpart of the ship.

Martin, Lancelot, and I hurried aft, where we found Dick lying on the deck, supported by a seaman, who seemed as wet as he was. We were told that the gallant fellow had fastened a rope round his waist, plunged overboard and picked up Dick just as he was being washed by astern. Dick quickly came to.

" Where is the boat ! " he asked, lifting up his head.

" She's gone to the bottom," answered Lancelot.

" Where are we ? "

" On board a ship."

" What ship, what ship ? " asked Dick, still confused.

" That's more than I can say," answered Lancelot, " We shall soon know, however."

CHAPTER IV.

SCARCELY were we on board the ship than the gale came down with greater fury than before, so that the seamen being required to hand the sails left us to ourselves. Two or three persons, however, gathered round us, one of whom — the surgeon, I concluded — advised that we should be taken below, and stripped of our wet clothes, for our teeth were chattering with the cold.

Very thankful to be so treated, we had no time to ask questions before we found ourselves in the officers' cabin; Dick and I being placed in one bed, and Lancelot in another, while Martin was allowed to go forward among the men, to obtain such assistance from them as they were inclined to give.

After a short time some food and a cup of warm tea were brought us, having partaken of which, thanks to its genial warmth, we soon fell asleep.

Once I awoke when the rolling and pitching, the battering of the sea against the sides, and the noises overhead, told me that the gale was still blowing. I was soon asleep

"HALLOA, YOUNG MASTERS, WHO ARE YOU?"

again, and when I opened my eyes it was broad daylight.
No one was in the cabin. I roused my companions. Our
clothes had been brought back tolerably well dried, so we
dressed, intending to go on deck and learn what ship we
were on board of, and where we were bound.

The pistols, hangers, and other weapons hanging up
against the bulkhead showed us she was a ship of war, and
Lancelot discovered several prints ornamenting his cabin,
which made us suspect that she did not belong to the
Puritans.

"If they inquire who we are, as they are sure to do, what
shall we say about ourselves?" asked Dick.

"Tell the truth and shame the devil! Whoever they are,
we should be grateful to them for having saved our lives,
and maybe, if we speak them fair, they'll set us on shore
at the first port they touch at," answered Lancelot.

"If they're Cavaliers, there's no port they can put into
on the south coast without the certainty of being fired at,"
I observed, "though perhaps they may be induced to set
us ashore in one of their boats, and we can find our way
back over land. I much wish to relieve the anxiety that
Audrey and Cicely and your father must be feeling about
us, for they will—should we not return—give us up for lost."

"We shan't grow wiser by staying here," said Lancelot,
as he led the way on deck.

"Halloa, young masters. Who are you?" exclaimed a
gentleman in plumed hat, scarlet doublet, and sword hanging by a rich scarf at his side.

An officer approached and spoke to the gentleman, whom
we guessed must be the captain.

I had time to look around; the sea had somewhat
gone down, but it was still blowing fresh. Over the starboard quarter I observed a long point, which I at first
thought was the Start, but afterwards learned was the

Lizard. The frigate, for such I saw was the vessel we were
on board of, was heeling over to the breeze, and the Union
Jack waving from her peak showed me that she belonged
to the Royalist party; indeed, when I remarked the varied
costumes of the officers, the careless manners of the crew,
and heard their strange oaths, I had no doubt about the
matter.

Seeing that we were expected to reply to the question
put to us, Lancelot advanced and informed the captain that
we were young gentlemen belonging to Lyme, and were
taking a pleasure trip when caught by the gale.

"Young Roundheads, I wot," answered the captain, with
an oath. "You might have been left to drown with small
loss to honest men. However, as you are now on board the
frigate, you may remain, and we will see to what use we
can put you. You have a companion, I understand. Is
he a sailor?"

"Yes!" I answered, somewhat incautiously. "He spent
his early life at sea, and visited many strange parts with
my late father, Captain Bracewell."

"So much the better for him. He shall serve on board,
and I will order his name to be entered on the books."

From the way we were first received, we fancied that we
should have been treated like young gentlemen, but on his
ordering us with an oath to go forward and do what we
were told, such we found was not the captain's intention. We
obeyed, for we had no choice. On our way we encountered
a big fellow with a knotted rope in his hand, who, from the
chain with a whistle hanging to it round his neck, we knew
was the boatswain.

"Come along, my young masters. I'll soon find tasks
for you. You!" he exclaimed, seizing Dick, "go and help
the cook in the galley, you two will pick oakum," he added,
turning to Lancelot and me; "and when the hands are

sent aloft to reef sails, as you seem active fellows, you'll go
to the foretop-gallant yard."

"But I have never been aloft," said Lancelot, "and
shan't know what to do when I get there."

"Then the sooner you go the faster you'll learn, or you'll
have a taste of my persuader," and he flourished the knotted
rope. "Up, both of you, and let me see how you can lay
out on the yard."

As we hesitated, flourishing the rope, he laid it across
our shoulders, at which the men standing by laughed and
jeered at us. To remonstrate was useless, so to avoid a re-
petition of the unpleasant infliction, we sprang into the
rigging and began to mount, taking care to hold tight as we
went up until we got into the top, where we both stood
looking down, not liking to go higher.

"Aloft with you, aloft, or I'll send a couple of hands to
start you," shouted the boatswain from the deck.

We looked up at the tall mast swaying to and fro, and I
fully expected, should I make the attempt, to fall down on
deck, or to be plunged into the sea, for which I had no
wish ; but looking down for a moment, and seeing two men
about to come up the rigging, I told Lancelot that I would
run the chance.

"It is the only thing we can do," he answered.

Catching hold of the topmast shrouds, we began to
mount. We got up at length, and crawled out on the yard,
holding on tightly by the ropes which seemed most secure.
Finding that it was not so terrible as I had supposed,
I crawled out to the very end of the yard, where I
clung on, in spite of the fearful way in which it moved
about.

Thankful I was, however, to hear the boatswain shout,
"You may come down now, lads ;" and I made my way
into the top.

Lancelot had gone out at the other end of the yard, and when we met on deck he could not help shaking hands, as if we had arrived successfully from some desperate enterprise. The seamen laughed as they saw us, and even the boatswain's grim features wrinkled into a smile.

"You'll do, lads," he said. "You'll make prime topmen in a few weeks, and thank me for having taught you."

Such was the commencement of our sea life. Things, we agreed, might have been worse, though we got many a kick and rope's ending, not only from the boatswain, but from others among the more brutal of the crew.

Martin, when on deck, always came to our rescue, but old as he was, he was but ill able to contend with so many opposed to him.

"Better grin and bear it, Master Ben," he said; "they'll soon give up ill-treating you if you take it with good temper, and I should do more harm than good if I was to shove in my oar except at a favourable time; but I shall be on the watch, never fear, and I'll take care matters don't grow too bad."

We followed Martin's advice, and found it answer. The seamen of the frigate were a lawless and disorderly set, every sentence they uttered being accompanied by strange oaths, while below, when not asleep, they spent their time in dicing and gaming.

We found, I should have said, that we were on board the *Charles* frigate, Captain Blackleach, carrying one hundred and fifty men and thirty-two guns, one of Prince Rupert's squadron, from which she had been separated while in chase of a trader the captain had hoped to capture, but which had escaped.

A bright look-out was now kept for the squadron, and for traders of all nations.

Our cruising ground was the mouth of the English

Channel, where wo lay in wait to pounce down upon any unwary vessel coming up with a rich cargo.

We were all three below, poor Dick by this time looking as black as a negro ; he had unfortunately let it be known whose son he was, and consequently, I believe, got a double allowance of ill-treatment.

" All hands make sail ! " was shouted, and we with the rest sprang on deck.

" Aloft, you youngsters ! " cried the boatswain, looking at Lancelot and me.

We ran up the rigging to the fore-top gallant-yard, and with the aid of two other men let fall the sail which had been furled.

On looking ahead, we saw a large ship in the distance, for which the frigate was steering. The stranger held on her course, not apparently fearing us, though we had the Union Jack flying at the peak, while that of Holland fluttered at hers.

On getting within range of our guns, we opened fire from a dozen pieces or more, but without doing her much damage. Again we fired, sending our shot crashing on board her, when the guns being run in and reloaded, we stood on, receiving her broadside, the shots going through our sails and cutting some of our running rigging, then luffing up across her bows, we raked her fore and aft, and went about, showing that we intended to give her the other broadside. Not relishing this, she hauled down her colours and triced up her sails.

A well-armed boat's crew was sent on board to take possession, when her ship's company were speedily removed, and those of her people who remained in her were ordered to steer her to Kinsale harbour, a short distance to the southward of Cork, in Ireland.

The next vessel we chased proved to be English, and as

she was bound for the Thames, she was captured and sent away like the first, with part of the Dutch crew, who, being promised good pay, had no objection to navigate her.

A third vessel was seen the next day, carrying the flag of France. Chase was given to her also, and the *Charles* coming alongside, she struck without firing a shot. She was also sent away, under command of one of the officers, for the same harbour as the former prize.

"Why, these fellows are pirates," observed Lancelot to me, though he took care to speak in a low voice, so that only Martin and I who was standing near could hear him.

"Little doubt about that," answered Martin; "all's fish that comes to their net! I wish that we were well free of them, but how to get away is the difficulty. I suspect that if a Parliamentary ship was to catch the frigate, they'd hang us all up at the yard-arms."

"Heaven forbid!" said Lancelot.

A few days after this, the look-out from the mast-head shouted—

"Five sail to the eastward!"

Presently afterwards three more were seen standing down channel, under all the canvas they could carry.

"What if they should prove to be Parliamentary ships," I said to Lancelot.

"We must try and explain who we are, and how we came on board," he answered.

"But what if they won't believe us?" I asked. "We may be strung up before they find out the truth."

"That would be a hard case, but I do not see how we are to escape, unless we jump overboard when the fight begins, and try to swim to one of them."

Instead of running away, as we expected, the *Charles* stood boldly towards the approaching squadron. At length from the peak of the leading ship we saw the Union Jack flying.

"That must be Prince Rupert's squadron after all," said Lancelot.

That this was the case was soon evident, for the frigate, ranging up alongside the big ship, exchanged friendly salutes.

An officer in handsome costume, with a gold chain round his neck, was seen standing on the after castle. When Captain Blackleach raised his beaver, the officer took off his in return, and inquired how many prizes he had made.

"Three since we parted with your highness," was the answer, "and they are by this time safe in Kinsale harbour."

"You have used diligence; you shall have a bigger ship before long," said the officer in the handsome dress.

"Who is he?" I asked one of the men standing by.

"What! have you never seen Prince Rupert, the bravest commander in the king's armies, and now his best admiral? Wherever he leads, rich prizes are sure to be found."

Such we discovered was a fact, for that very day the squadron captured well-nigh a dozen merchantmen homeward bound, which mistook it for the Earl of Warwick's fleet, and fell without firing a shot into its voracious jaws.

In high glee the Prince with his prizes stood for Kinsale harbour, where we found a dozen other goodly ships, which had been captured by his cruisers, including the three taken by the *Charles*. While we lay here, Lancelot and I, when no one was by, often talked over various schemes for escaping, but we had to ask ourselves the question, where should we go? The whole southern part of Ireland was in favour of the King, as the Prince of Wales was now called, his father having been put to death in London. Thus, even should we reach the shore, we should run a great risk of being knocked on the head when attempting to travel through the country, for rumours had reached us of the fearful way in which the Romanists had treated the Protestants residing among them.

Martin to whom we confided our wishes, was as eager as we were to escape, being anxious, as he said, to get away from the swearing, drinking, gambling crew. "I won't say there's not a godly man among them, because there are two or three who have been pressed into the service, and are ready to get away if they can, but the rest, the Lord deliver us from them," he said, while we were standing on the forecastle one evening, out of hearing of the rest of the ship's company.

Lancelot, who was full of devices, proposed that we should take a boat and pull away out to sea, hoping that we might get across to the Welsh coast and be picked up by a Parliamentary cruiser, some of which were said to be in the Irish Channel.

This plan seemed most feasible, though in reality full of danger. It would be no easy matter, in the first place, to get hold of a boat, and to obtain provisions and water. It would be still more difficult to slip away out of the harbour unperceived; and then, after all, we might be picked up by one of Prince Rupert's squadron and treated as deserters.

"Nothing risk, nothing have!" said Martin. "I would chance it for myself, but I do not like the thought of hazarding your young lives. Howsumdever, I'll speak to the men I think will join us, and hear what they say."

The *Charles* was one of the outer line of frigates placed at the entrance of the harbour to give due notice of the approach of an enemy, so that we should have a better opportunity of getting off than would have been the case had we been higher up the harbour; but then the difficulty of obtaining a boat was greater.

Many of the crew were allowed to go on shore, but we had hitherto always been refused. Lancelot suggested that if we could by some means get on shore, we might obtain a boat, and late in the evening pretend to be returning in her to the ship, instead of which we might pass her and get out to sea.

"I fear that the guard ships keep too sharp a look-out to allow us to do that," observed Martin; "still, I see no better way of making our escape."

"We must wait for our opportunity; it will come, maybe, when we least expect it," said Lancelot.

Buoyed up with this hope, when our watch was over, we turned into our hammocks.

Next morning a frigate came in, towing a boat. She passed close to us. On her deck stood ten men heavily ironed, their features, which we could clearly see, showing that they felt themselves to be in a dangerous predicament. The frigate sailed on, and brought up in the centre of the squadron.

Soon afterwards a signal from the flag ship was seen flying, ordering two boats from each vessel to come along-side. Ours were in the water, when the captain ordered Martin and three other men, together with Lancelot, Dick, and me, to go in one of them.

"It may teach you a lesson, lads, which for your own sakes I advise you not to forget," he said with a significant look.

"I am afraid the captain has an inkling of our plans," whispered Lancelot to me as we went down the side.

We took our seats in our respective boats, which pulled away up the harbour. We found numerous other boats, the men resting on their oars round the flag-ship. Presently a gun was fired from her, and up went ten human beings dangling by their necks to the yard-arms. Some struggled in a way it was fearful to look at. They were the men we had seen on the deck of the frigate, and who had, we heard, attempted to make their escape in a boat, just as we proposed doing. Such would have been our fate had we carried out our intention and been captured.

We returned on board very low-spirited.

"We must be careful what we are about," said Lancelot to me; "I have no fancy to share the lot of those unhappy fellows."

"What's to be done?" I asked.

"Grin and bear it, as Martin would say," he answered.

Although we were not allowed to go on shore, we saw what was taking place up the harbour. Boats were constantly going backwards and forwards, carrying the cargoes of the captured vessels to the town, where the goods were disposed of to eager traders, who came in from all parts to purchase them—often for less than half their value; but still, from the number of vessels taken, they must have realised a large profit to the Prince, seeing that he had paid nothing for them.

The cargoes being discharged, the stouter ships were fitted out with guns, there being found no lack of men ready to serve under so successful a corsair, for such the Prince had become.

The fleet being ready, we once more sailed in quest of fresh prizes. I did not note the number taken, but I often grieved to see the despair of the poor ship-masters and owners when they found themselves robbed of their hard-earned gains. No flag protected them — Dutchmen, Spaniards, Portuguese, Englishmen, all were treated alike. Some fought pretty hard, especially the English, but the frigates hung about them, preventing their escape, until the big ships came down and they were compelled to strike their flags.

We were cruising about the mouth of the Channel, and, favoured by fine weather, had taken many prizes, when a south-westerly wind sprang up, and soon increased to a heavy gale, harder than any we had yet encountered.

The dark leaden seas came rolling up from the Atlantic, crested with foam, which flew in masses across our decks. The sky, covered with black clouds, sent forth vivid flashes of lightning, whilst peals of rattling thunder vied with the loud howling of the blast through the rigging, the creaking of blocks and bulkheads, and the dashing of the waves against the bows and sides. Now the wind blew from one quarter, now from another, and prevented our running for Kinsale, the only harbour in which we could have found a secure refuge.

We could see the rest of the fleet tumbling and tossing about under close-reefed canvas, scattered far and wide, some in one direction, some in another. Thus the night closed down upon us. We had to keep a watchful eye on every side, for should we run foul of another ship under such circumstances, the destruction of both would be inevitable.

The next day and the greater part of the following night the storm raged with as much fury as ever. Fearful of being driven on the Scilly Isles, or the southern coast of England, our captain endeavoured to keep a good offing, though we thereby lost sight of the rest of the fleet. About the middle of the next night the storm began to abate, and when morning came we found ourselves enveloped in a thick fog, while the ocean, though still heaving in slow undulations, gradually assumed a glass-like surface of leaden hue.

We, having borne up, stood to the northward in search of the squadron. The captain ordered a bright look-out to be kept.

"Marry! a bright look-out. We must have eyes of a different nature to most men to pierce through this dense mist," quoth Martin, laughing.

Still, such a look-out as was possible was kept, the
captain hoping ere long to see one of the Prince's vessels,
and to learn from her where the rest were to be found.
At length, about noon, the sun made an effort to burst
through the thick veil which shrouded us. Soon afterwards the mist lifted for an instant ahead, and during that
instant I saw what appeared to me the hull of a ship, the
canvas just rising above it; but it was only a glimpse, and
it needed a sharp pair of eyes to discern any object a few
fathoms off. I pointed her out to Lancelot, but he was
doubtful whether I had actually seen a vessel, and no one
else appeared to have observed her. The frigate therefore
stood on, and unless the stranger which I supposed I had
seen was sailing at equal speed, we must have passed her
to leeward. Presently the wind blowing stronger, the fog
once more lifted, and the sun bursting through, it fell on
the white canvas of a tall ship close aboard us to windward.

Putting up her helm, she came nearer, when the captain
hailed through his trumpet, supposing her to be one of
Prince Rupert's squadron. The answer was not heard, but
the question, "What ship is that?" came down clearly to us.

"The *Charles*," answered the captain, again putting the
same question.

Scarcely had he spoken than we heard the words, "Strike
to the Parliament ship, *Constant Warwick!*" and, the mist
clearing still more, we saw flying from her peak a white
flag with a red cross.

"We are caught in a trap, and must fight to get out of
it," exclaimed the captain, ordering the drums to beat to
quarters.

The men rushed to the guns, which they were well
accustomed to handle; but before they could cast off the
lashings and run them out, a broadside from the *Constant*

Warwick came crashing into us, several of the crew being struck to the deck to rise no more. With scant ceremony their shipmates hove the bodies overboard, while the gunners, running out their pieces, returned with interest the fire of the other frigate.

I prayed that neither my friends nor I might be killed or wounded, though we ran as great a risk as the rest. I felt thankful when we were all three ordered down to the magazine to bring up powder, for below the risk of being hit was less, though neither of us felt any cowardly fears.

Having brought up the powder, we were ordered to sit on the tubs until it was wanted. We could thus see what was going forward, though we would far rather, I must confess, have been below. Captain Blackleach, a brave fellow, to give him his due, seemed in no way inclined to strike while he had a chance of getting off. The *Constant Warwick's* fore-yard was soon shot away, and her main top-mast shortly afterwards fell, on which our corsair crew cheered lustily, and with redoubled vigour plied their guns. I looked round to see how it was faring with my friends, Dick and Lancelot. They were seated on their tubs, Dick making himself as small as possible, so as to have less chance of being hit. A short way off stood Martin Shobbrok among the sail trimmers. Just then two of the gunners fell, their heads shot off, and their brains scattered over the deck. The captain, seeing what had occurred, shouted to Martin and another man to take their places. Martin stood with his arms folded, as if he did not hear the order. The captain again shouted to him.

"I'll do a seaman's duty, but will not fight against those who have justice and right on their side," answered Martin.

"Mutiny! mutiny!" shouted the captain. "Suffer the

fate of a mutineer!" and, drawing a pistol from his belt he fired.

I expected to see my old friend fall, but the bullet merely grazed one of his grey whiskers; and, fixing his eye on the captain, he answered—

"The Lord forgive thee, and be thankful thou hast not murdered an old man who is acting as his conscience bids him."

The captain, unmoved by this rebuke, was about to draw another pistol.

"I must save Martin, even at the hazard of my own life," I exclaimed, and was about to spring aft to strike up the pistol when the cry arose—

"Another enemy close aboard us!"

Looking round, I saw, looming large through the fog, the wide-spread canvas of a tall ship coming up on our quarter.

CHAPTER V.

THE ENGAGEMENT.

THE fate of honest Martin hung in the balance; should I fail to strike up the captain's arm, his death would be certain. Whether or no my action had been observed I could not tell, for the appearance of the stranger drew the captain's attention off from his victim, and in a moment he seemed to have forgotten all about Martin.

The approaching ship fired a broadside which raked us fore and aft, sending many of the roystering crew to their dread account. Still undaunted, the captain ordered the starboard broadside to be fired in return, and the *Constant Warwick*, in consequence of the loss of her head-sail, being unable to keep her position, we drew ahead of her; but our fresh antagonist, with her yards and rigging uninjured, quickly came up, and her guns, aimed at our masts, ere long brought down the fore and main yards; but the flag still flew out at the peak of the corsair, and her guns on either side continued to belch forth their deadly missiles.

Though round shot and bullets from her antagonists came crashing on board the ship, tearing up the decks, piercing the sides, carrying away lanterns, boats, and spars, wounding her masts and plunging through her bulwarks, the scuppers running with blood, her gallant captain, standing still unharmed amid the dead and dying, refused to yield.

Malignant though he was, I could not help admiring his courage, regretting that he was not fighting in a better cause. I heartily wished that he would give in before more damage was done.

He seemed, however, in no way inclined to strike while there was a chance of escaping.

I feared, indeed, that after all he would get off, but the two Parliament ships plied him hard. Their commanders were as brave as he was, and had no intention of letting him escape.

Of this the corsair's crew were at length convinced, and some, unwilling to encounter certain destruction, cried out to strike the flag.

"Who dares to say that?" shouted Captain Blackleach. Then he cried out to the boatswain, "Reeve a dozen ropes, and we'll show our enemies how we treat traitors to our cause."

The boatswain, seizing one of the men who desired to strike, was actually about to put the order into execution when Martin rushed to the poor fellow's rescue.

"Avast, master boatswain!" he exclaimed, cutting the rope; "are you not afraid of committing murder, when, at any moment, you may be sent to stand before the Judge of all men?"

The boatswain, with an oath, again seized the man, and,

AN AWKWARD POSITION.

aided by his mates, was forming a noose at the end of a rope, when a shot striking him on the breast sent his mangled body through a wide gap in the bulwarks into the blood-stained ocean. Most of the superior officers had by this time been killed or wounded, the latter being in the hands of the surgeon below.

" What's to be done?" said Dick, as we were together making our way to the magazine, being ordered down to fetch up more powder. "Surely the captain won't hold out longer. If I didn't feel that it was cowardly, I should like to stow myself away below till all is over."

"To go down with the ship and be drowned," I observed.

"No, no; let us remain on deck while we can, and take our chance," said Lancelot. " If the captain fights on until the ship sinks, we may get hold of a plank or spar. The Roundhead seamen will not let us drown, even though they think we are Malignants."

"Stay for me!" said Dick, as he saw us lifting up our tubs to go on deck again. To say the truth, I suspected that he had been in no hurry to fill his.

Just as we were going up the ladder two thundering broadsides sounded in our ears, and several shot, crashing through the stout planks and scattering splinters in every direction, passed close to our heads, but happily none of us were hit. They were followed by the groans and shrieks of the wounded as they lay struggling on the deck in their agony. Then there came what truly seemed an awful silence. We had naturally stopped midway on the ladder for unwilling slaves as we were, we lacked a motive to expedite our movements.

As we at length gained the upper deck a sound of cheering struck on our ears, but it came from the other ships. I looked up at the peak. The flag was no longer there. On the after-castle lay the captain; he had fallen desperately wounded. Two officers alone remained on their feet, while fore and aft a sickening sight met our view. The ship was a perfect shambles ; the dead and dying lay everywhere, the countenances of many distorted with agony ; the decks slippery with blood, and covered with blocks, ropes, torn canvas, and shattered spars, while several guns had been dismounted, and every boat knocked to pieces. The master of the mariners, one of the surviving officers, was shouting to the crew to shorten sail.

Throwing our tubs of powder on deck, we gladly ran to obey the order, joined by Martin Shobbrok, who, amid the bloody strife, had escaped unscathed.

Meantime the two victorious frigates had hove to and were lowering their boats, ready to send on board and take possession of their prize.

" What shall we do now ? " asked Dick, as the boats were coming alongside. " Our friends will look upon us as deserters, and perhaps string us up at the yard-arm."

" Not much fear of that," said Lancelot. " We can tell who we are and how we came to be on board."

" But will they believe us ? " asked Dick. " The rest of the crew will prove that we have been helping the gunners to load their pieces by bringing powder from the magazine."

" Just trust in God, young masters," said Martin, who had overheard them.

We had not much time for talking before the crews of the three boats which had been sent sprang on board. The officer in command at once ordered the whole of the " rovers " to muster aft. Of well-nigh two hundred men who had commenced the action, one half were dead or wounded. The survivors stood with downcast looks, expecting no gentle treatment.

" You have taken up arms without lawful authority against the Parliament, and you must be prepared for the punishment due to you, unless the admiral thinks fit to remit it," explained the officer, casting his eye over the men. "Have you anything to say for yourselves?"

There was no reply until Lancelot stepped aft, followed by Martin, Dick, and me.

"We were on board against our will, sir," he said, "and acknowledge the Parliament as the supreme authority in the realm." He then described how we had been rescued by the *Charles* when on our way from Dartmouth to Lyme.

"A likely story, young master," said the officer; "but I will talk to you more anon. The rest of you tumble into the boats and go peaceably on board the ships to which they will convey you."

Nearly half the men had already taken their seats in the three boats which had shoved off, when the cry arose, "The ship is sinking!"

The carpenter and his mates were among those who remained, and the officer ordering some of his own men to assist them in stopping the leaks, directed them to man the pumps. The rovers obeyed with alacrity, for they had no wish to drown.

We four assisted them, and as the pumps clanged loudly the water spread over the decks, partly cleansing them from their bloody stains.

It was an anxious time, for I feared that the ship would go down before the boats could return. We pumped, and pumped away with might and main, while the carpenters stopped the most dangerous shot holes between wind and water.

It was a great relief at length to see the boats come back. They brought more men, and among them some carpenters from the frigates to assist in repairing the damages. The remaining prisoners having laboured so well, had the choice given them of continuing on board, and they gladly accepted the offer, promising faithfully to serve the Parliament.

Evening was drawing on, and the two frigates lay still hove to close to the prize, when, looking to windward, I saw the upper sails of several ships, which I deemed to be of size, rising above the horizon. I pointed them out to Martin, and asked if he thought they were Prince Rupert's squadron.

"No fear of that," he answered; "they must have been seen some time ago from the frigate, and they show no intention of trying to escape."

During this time everyone on board was working away with a will, for there was much to be done both below and aloft, while the wounded men had to be looked after.

The captain had been taken to his cabin, where the surgeon had dressed his wound. Dick, who had been ordered to watch him, came rushing out after some time, looking greatly terrified, and declared that the captain was raving and swearing that he would rise and blow up the ship rather than yield to the Roundheads.

Fortunately we found the surgeon, who sent two men to watch over him, and Dick was relieved from his trying duty. A boat now came alongside with orders to remove more of the prisoners, and among them Martin and my two friends and I were ordered to get into her. In a short time we were conveyed on board the *Constant Warwick*, and found ourselves standing on her deck together with the other prisoners.

"Now is our time," I exclaimed to Lancelot. "Let us go boldly aft and tell the captain who we are, or we shall be sent below and placed in irons with the rest."

Lancelot took my advice. We stepped aft, followed by Dick and Martin.

"What have you to say, lads?" asked the captain, looking greatly astonished at our audacity.

We gave him the same account of ourselves that we had to the officer who had come on board the *Charles*.

"You are ready enough now to declare yourselves Roundheads," answered the captain, "but you were found on board an enemy's ship, and must be treated like the rest."

"They are brave little fighting-cocks, Cavaliers to the backbone," shouted one of the men from the group of prisoners, not wishing that we should receive more favour than themselves.

I had observed a young officer standing close to the captain. I looked at his countenance, and the thought flashed across me that I had seen him before.

"Captain Stayner," he said, "allow me to say that I believe the account these young gentlemen give of themselves. I was at Lyme with my uncle, the admiral;" then turning to us he inquired our names.

"I thought so," he said, putting out his hand; "I remember them all well. One is the son of Mr. Kerridge, the mayor, who fought so bravely for the good cause; the father of the other, who served under my grandfather, was killed during the siege; and this one," he added, taking Dick by the hand, "is the son of Mr. Harvey, who expended his means in aiding in the defence of Lyme."

While the young officer was speaking, I recognised him as the nephew of Colonel Blake. "I truly rejoice to see you," he continued, turning to us, "for, putting into Lyme some weeks ago, I found your relatives and friends in great sorrow at your supposed loss. We will take the earliest opportunity of sending them news of your safety."

Thus were our anxieties brought to an end. Instead of being treated as prisoners, we were received as guests by the officers, who insisted on supplying us with clothes and other necessaries, of which we stood much in want. Great was our surprise to hear that the admiral of the ships in sight astern was no other than Colonel Blake, who had been placed in command of the fleets of England by the Parliament in conjunction with Colonels Deane and Popham.

Admiral Blake was now in chase of Prince Rupert's squadron, which it was his intention, should he fail to overtake it at sea, to shut up in Kinsale harbour. This, to me especially, was satisfactory news, for I had not forgotten the remark made by Colonel Blake to my father, that he should like to have me with him, and I felt very sure that he was a man who would fulfil his intentions.

I mentioned this to Mr. Robert Blake, who promised on the first opportunity to take me on board the flagship and introduce me to the admiral.

"Not that you will require an introduction," he answered; "my uncle never forgets those he has once known, and, though grown, you are not altered much from the little fellow I remember at Lyme."

I felt bound to put in a word for my two friends, as also for Martin, whose brave conduct on board the *Charles* I described, when he refused to fire at the *Constant Warwick*.

"It would not become me to make promises to you," he replied, "but you may depend upon it that the admiral will not overlook such conduct, and as Shobbrok is an experienced seaman, he will gladly place him in some position of trust on board."

The other frigate which had assisted in the capture of the *Charles* was, I should have said, the *Seaford*. The breeze freshening, we had no opportunity of going on board the *Triumph*, Admiral Blake's flag-ship, as he was pressing on under all sail in chase of the corsairs. The frigates led the way, and the next morning, from the masthead of the *Constant Warwick*, we caught sight of well-nigh a score of ships right ahead. That they were those of Prince Rupert we had no doubt; but they must have seen us coming, and having no stomach to engage in fight—for they knew by this time who commanded the English fleet—they pressed on before us.

We continued in chase under every stitch of canvas we could carry, hoping to come up with one or more of the rearmost ships and to bring them to action, so as to keep them employed till the rest of the fleet should arrive and compel them to strike. The breeze freshened, and the *Constant Warwick*, followed closely by two other frigates, tore through the water, as if eager to overtake her foes.

" Hold on, good sticks!" cried the captain, looking aloft. "Time enough to go overboard when we have grappled the enemy."

The top-gallant masts bent like willow wands, and I expected every moment to see them fall, but though the lofty sails tugged and tugged, yet they held fast, and we hoped that we should yet be in time to stop some of the corsairs before they could get into harbour. The *Triumph* was still far away astern, followed by the rest of the fleet, our captain doing his best to drive his ship through the water. The corsairs did not gain upon us, and we well knew that for a good hour or more we should have them to ourselves, should we overtake them. Captain Stayner walked the deck, now casting his eye ahead at the enemy, now aloft at the straining canvas, and now astern, to judge, by the way the sails of the *Triumph* were blowing out, how the wind was holding in that direction. Presently the lofty canvas was seen to hang down against the masts, then slowly to blow out again. In a short time our own royals and top-gallant sails followed their bad example. The captain gave a stamp of impatience on the deck. The breeze was falling, even the top-sails and courses no longer bellied out as before. Still, the frigates glided on, but the sluggish eddies astern showed how greatly their speed had decreased.

At length, on the larboard bow, the old head of Kinsale appeared in sight, with Prince Rupert's ships passing round it. Still, they too might get becalmed and a change of wind enable us to approach them. Our hopes, however, were doomed to be disappointed. Though the wind was light, they moved as fast as we did, and the lighter vessels getting out their sweeps, they ere long disappeared, shrouded by the gloom of evening, and by the time we came off the mouth of the harbour not a sail was to be discerned.

"Though they have escaped us this time, we have shut the rats up in their hole, and they will find it a hard matter to get out again to seek for prey," observed the captain.

"Can't we go in and destroy them?" inquired Lancelot of Mr. Blake.

"From the information we have received, we judge that it would be a hazardous undertaking," he answered. "There are castles on either side of the harbour, and the corsairs have thrown up earthworks, armed with heavy guns, for the protection of their ships, so that they would blow us out of the water should we attempt to enter. We must content ourselves with blockading them."

Such. I afterwards found, was the plan adopted. We stood on and off the land to watch the entrance. The next morning the whole fleet arrived, forming a line from the old head of Kinsale northward, which Prince Rupert, daring as he was, would not, it was believed, attempt to break through. It was somewhat trying work. Night and day a vigilant watch was kept, great care being

required so that each ship should maintain her proper
position, and that one should not run foul of the other.

According to his promise, Mr. Blake took Lancelot, Dick,
and me, with Martin Shobbrok, on board the *Triumph.*
The admiral recognised me immediately, and remembered
also what he had said to my father.

"Would you wish to remain with me?" he asked.
"Should such be your desire, you shall become my cabin
boy, and when you have gained a knowledge of navigation
and seamanship, you shall, without delay, be made an
officer."

"Such I desire above all things," I answered, "and I
am deeply grateful for the offer."

"And your friends here," he continued, looking at
Lancelot and Dick. Were they with us at the siege
of Lyme?"

"They were, sir, and we all three worked together
to throw up the embankments," I answered.

"Good! they appear likely lads, and I will watch
over their interests, if the Lord spares my life."

Lancelot and Dick made proper acknowledgment of the
admiral's intended kindness. I then bethought me that
now was the time to speak a word for Martin, and told the
admiral how he had behaved on board the *Charles,* being
ready to lose his own life rather than fire at the Parliamentary ships.

"Brave fellow! I remember him when he served with
your father and mine," he observed. "He shall have a
post on board such as his merit deserves. I will see
to it."

Several captains from other ships coming on board,
we retired, following young Robert Blake, who took us
into the gun room, where he introduced us to such of
the officers of the ship as were below.

I had long been wishing to hear from Lieutenant Blake
how his uncle had become an admiral, and I now took the
opportunity of asking him.

" Simply because he is one of the most worthy men the
Parliament could find." he answered.   " His great talents,
his undaunted bravery, are well known, and although he
had not before been to sea, the Government felt sure
that he would be able to fill the post, and seeing him
as we do now at the head of naval affairs, no one would
suppose that he was fifty years of age before he set his
foot on the deck of a ship as commander, taking precedence
of such men as Captains Penn, Jordan, Ascue, Stayner,
and Lawson, while Admirals Deane and Popham, though
of the same rank, yield to his judgment."

For the benefit of those who may not be acquainted with
the history of one of the most famous of England's sea
commanders, I may here note that Admiral Blake, eldest
son of a highly-esteemed merchant, Humphrey Blake,
trading with Spain and other foreign parts, was born
at Bridgwater in the year of grace 1598, and that he
had many brothers and sisters.

When a boy he studied navigation and the routine of
sea duties from his father and some of his captains who
had come to live on shore, but at that time his own taste
made him wish to obtain a knowledge of literature, and at
sixteen he entered as an undergraduate at St. Alban's
Hall, Oxford, whence he removed to Wadham College.
Here he remained several years, until his father being
reduced in circumstances from the failure of many of his
enterprises, he returned home to watch over the interests
of his family.   He had, I should have said, offered himself
as a candidate for a scholarship then vacant at Merton, but
Sir Henry Saville, the warden, who delighted in tall men,
objecting to him on account of his height which fell below

his standard of manly perfection, refused to admit him, and the admiral, after he had been summoned to the death-bed of his father, did not again return to Oxford.

For some years he remained at Bridgwater, chiefly occupied with the care of his mother and brothers and sisters. At the same time he was a keen observer of passing events. His indignation was aroused by the persecutions of Bishop Laud and his attempt to impose the Papal system on his country. When the King, after a lapse of many years, summoned a parliament, the admiral, then Mr. Blake, went up as member for Bridgwater. Soon afterwards came the outbreak in Ireland, when forty thousand Protestants were murdered by the Papists, who asserted that the King sanctioned their bloody acts. Although this might not have been the case, the Parliament demanded that a fleet and army should be placed at their disposal to quell the rebels. Soon afterwards the King, leaving London, raised his standard at Northampton, and declared war against the Parliament and those who sided with it. Mr. Blake was among the first gentlemen who took up arms in the south of England in defence of the people's right, his first military achievement being the gallant defence of Prior's Hill, Bristol. The rest of his career up to the time of which I am speaking I have already mentioned, and I may truly say that he had never been defeated. He had, for some time before I was received on board his flag-ship, been engaged in reforming the navy, into which numerous corruptions had crept. His great object was to see that the men were duly paid and well fed, that hospitals were provided for the wounded, and that stout seaworthy ships were alone employed. He perseveringly engaged even in the most minute details, to add to the comfort of his men, and already they had learned to trust and revere him. His fame had spread even among the Royalists, numbers of whom, escaping when opportunities occurred, eagerly came on board our ships to serve under his flag. That flag was now a red cross on a white ground, and that banner was destined soon to claim the respect of England's foes, wherever it was seen waving at the peak.

While we were watching Kinsale harbour to prevent the escape of Prince Rupert's cruisers, General Cromwell, who had gone over to the north of Ireland with an army, was fighting his way to the southward.

Blockading was no pleasant duty, for often heavy gales from the eastward compelled us to keep an offing from the shore, or when they blew from an opposite direction we had to beat backwards and forwards under close-reefed sails to maintain our position, and several times we had to run for Milford Haven, to escape the danger of shipwreck. We young seamen, however, thereby gained much practical experience in nautical affairs, as did undoubtedly our superiors, who had hitherto been more accustomed to the command of regiments of foot and horse than to the management of ships.

By the first bag of letters despatched after we got on board the *Triumph*, we wrote an account of our adventures to our friends at Lyme. In due course we received others in return, with expressions of thankfulness that we had escaped the perils to which we had been exposed.

Audrey and Cicely especially gave us an account of all that had occurred since we left home, praying that we might soon return.

October came, and with it a furious gale, which once more scattered the blockading squadron. In vain the *Triumph* endeavoured to maintain her station. Still she kept the sea in spite of the furious blasts which laid her over and threatened to carry away her masts and spars,

CHAPTER VII.

THE hopes of those who expected to return home were destined to be disappointed. We were still at sea, keeping a look-out for the fleet of the royal corsairs, when a shout from the mast-head announced the approach of several ships from the northward, and as they got nearer the white flag with the red cross flying from their peaks told us that they were friends.

The leading ship proved to be the *Fairfax*, of fifty-two guns and two hundred and fifty men, carrying the flag of Vice-Admiral Penn. Following her came the *Centurion*, Captain Lawson, the *Adventure*, Captain Ball, and two others commanded by Captains Howett and Jordan, with the *Assurance*, Captain Benjamin Blake, the younger brother of the admiral.

Directly afterwards Vice-Admiral Hall with another squadron of seven ships joined us. The admiral had now under him a fleet capable of coping with that of either

France or Spain.   His first object, however, was to capture
the corsairs, who were committing much damage among the
merchant vessels.   It was still unknown in what direction
they had gone, when, the day after Admiral Hall's squadron
had reached us, a vessel was seen coming from the south.

On approaching she hove to, and her master came on
board the flag-ship.   His vessel, he said, was the only one
which had escaped from Malaga, on the coast of Andalusia,
into which the corsairs had entered and burnt six of his
consorts under the very guns of the Spanish batteries.

" We shall catch them at last ! " exclaimed the admiral
on receiving this information, a gleam of satisfaction light-
ing up his countenance.

Having taken some stores on board which had just
arrived from England, we made sail for the Straits of
Gibraltar, Admiral Penn with his squadron being left to
watch outside the entrance to catch the corsairs, should they
endeavour to escape from the Mediterranean.   With a fair
wind we stood in for the gut, the lofty rock, on which we
could discern only a few ruins on our left, and the coast of
Africa on our right.

For centuries no English admiral's flag had been seen in
the Mediterranean, our merchant vessels trading in those
seas being thus exposed to the attacks of pirates without
hope of redress.   On coming off Malaga, we found to our
disappointment that the princes had fled, in what direction
no one would inform us.   While we lay there, a furious
gale threatened the destruction of our ships, but we rode it
out in safety.

Just as we were sailing, information was brought that
the pirates were in Cartagena.   Pressing on all sail, we
made for that port.   As we came off it, our hearts beat high
with satisfaction, for there lay the fleet for which we were
in search.

The admiral, who was well acquainted with the dilatoriness of Spanish diplomacy, not waiting for leave, bearing down on the corsairs attacked the *Roebuck*, the largest of their ships, and quickly mastered her.

Another was set on fire, while the remainder, cutting their cables, ran on shore utterly disabled. Great, however, was our disappointment not to find either of the princes; and we learned from some of the prisoners that they had both been separated from the rest of the squadron during the gale, but what had become of them we were unable to ascertain.

In vain we sailed from port to port. At last we heard that they had taken shelter in the harbour of Toulon. On receiving this information we immediately steered for that port. On arriving we found that the corsairs had been honourably received by the French admiral, and that assistance had been given to them to dispose of their plunder.

On this Admiral Blake sent word that he considered the French had been guilty of a hostile act, and that unless the corsairs were driven from the harbour, and the plunder restored to its lawful owners, he should feel justified in making reprisals on the commerce of France.

No answer was given to this message, but after a short time it was discovered that the two princes had fled, though in what direction we were, as before, unable to ascertain.

Leaving Admiral Penn to search for them, we at length steered for England. Just as we were passing through the Straits, a large ship was seen which approached us without any apparent hesitation, showing French colours. Getting nearer, she hove to, while a boat being lowered her captain came on board. He was received with the usual courtesy by the admiral in his cabin.

The Frenchman being seated, the admiral informed him

that he must consider himself a prisoner, and requested him to deliver up his sword.

"No, monsieur," answered the Frenchman; "not while I have strength to use it," and he placed his hand on the hilt.

"I confess, brave sir, that you have been unfairly beguiled on board, and that you were ignorant that I had thrown down the gauntlet to your admiral at Toulon. If you desire it, you may go on board your ship and try to escape if you have the power," said the admiral.

"I accept your generous offer," answered the Frenchman with a bow, and he made his way on deck. We attended him with due honour down the side, when he returned to his ship.

As soon as he had gone the drum beat to quarters, but we waited before firing, to allow him to prepare his own vessel for the encounter.

Due time having passed, we fired a shot across his bows, which he returned, aiming at the *Tiger*.

The fight now commenced in earnest. The Frenchmen fought bravely, endeavouring to knock away our spars so as to make their escape. But their gunnery was not equal to that of our men. So severely did we pound them, that after holding out two hours they hauled down their flag.

The boats were immediately sent to bring the prisoners on board, when the captain, making a low bow, bestowed an affectionate kiss on the hilt of his weapon, and handed it to the admiral, who replied—

"You are a brave man, and deserve to keep your sword: pray receive it and wear it for my sake," and he handed the weapon back to his prisoner.

The prize was a valuable acquisition, being a fine frigate of forty guns. Four other large French vessels were taken on our way home, and at length we arrived safely at Plymouth. Lancelot, Dick, and I at once got leave to go to Lyme, being anxious to learn whether any tidings had been received of the lost ones.

Mr. Harvey, who was there, received us very kindly. Every means had been taken for discovering them, but not even the slightest clue had been obtained, and he acknowledged that he had very slight hopes that we should ever again hear of them. The reality came with fearful force upon me when he said this, and it was with difficulty I could refrain from giving way to my passionate grief. Lancelot, feeling as I did there was nothing to keep us at home, returned to Plymouth, where Dick promised to follow.

On a bright day in the early part of spring, 1651, Lancelot and I went on board the *Tiger*, which had been hastily refitted for sea. Martin, who was on the look-out, welcomed us back.

"Just in time, gentlemen; there's work cut out for us, and the admiral is to be on board this evening," he said, as we shook hands. "We are to rout out that nest of hornets in Scilly, and I've a notion we shall make them disgorge the plunder they have been collecting for many years past."

We were truly thankful for the promised excitement, for in the present state of our minds we could ill brook idleness. Besides the *Tiger*, a number of small frigates were collected, well calculated for the work to be undertaken. The admiral, accompanied by his nephew, came on board that evening, the former receiving Lancelot and me in his usual kind way, not forgetting to make inquiries whether our sisters and his friend Mr. Kerridge had returned. "Don't despair, notwithstanding, my young friends," he said, when we told him nothing had been heard of them. "By God's providence they may still be found."

Robert had now become, next to the captain, the principal officer on board, and though so young, he well fulfilled the duties of his post.

Lancelot had been promoted to the rank of lieutenant, but Dick and I were still in the admiral's cabin. We were often employed in transcribing his letters and other similar duties, though at the same time we pursued our nautical studies. Despatches being received from London, we immediately sailed for our destination. Two days' sail brought us in sight of the Scilly Islands, slumbering quietly on the surface of the bright blue ocean. They looked green and pleasant to the eye, with here and there a few rocky heights rising in their midst, but in most parts the land was not elevated many feet above the water. Above the other hills appeared the height on whose summit the Cavaliers had built a strong castle, which it was our object to capture. Coming off St. Mary's, the principal island, we hove to, and the admiral ordered a boat to be lowered, in which went Robert Blake, and I accompanied him, bearing a message summoning Sir John Grenville, the governor, to surrender. Having proceeded up the channel leading to the fort, we landed, bearing a white flag, and walked on until we reached the entrance. We were at once admitted, when we had an opportunity of taking a glance round the fortifications. The castle was filled with men, a large number being evidently, from their dress and appearance, officers. They were rollicking-looking gentlemen, and were laughing, and joking, and amusing themselves at our expense as we passed along.

Sir John Grenville received us with due courtesy. On reading the summons he replied—

"I might rather demand that Admiral Blake should deliver up his fleet, but yet I am willing to enter into a treaty, although it should be known to you that I have a

SUMMONS TO SURRENDER.

force with me not only sufficient to protect these islands, but to restore the exiled prince to the throne of his fathers."

"The result will prove that, sir," answered the young lieutenant. "Am I to inform the admiral that you refuse to deliver up the islands and their castles to the fleet of the Commonwealth?"

"Certainly such is my intention," answered Sir John, and he bowed us out of the hall.

We returned unmolested to the boat, and pulled back for the ship. No sooner had we arrived than the admiral sent for Captain Morris, one of the most trusted of his commanders, and ordered him to take eight hundred of the best men from the different ships, and to land at the back of Tresco, which is next in size to St. Mary's, and lies close to it.

Lieutenant Blake and I, with a small body of seamen from our ship, accompanied the troops. We found a line of breastworks thrown up for the defence of the shore, and held by fully a thousand men. But our brave leader was not to be hindered in performing his duty by this show of resistance. The boats in line dashed on, and in spite of the round shot plunged in among us, and the bullets whistling about our ears, the moment the keels touched the beach we threw ourselves overboard, and, wading on shore, speedily formed. Then the order to advance was given, and pike in hand we rushed up the bank. The Cavaliers received us with a hot fire of musketry, but their artillery was silent, being unable to play on us without hitting them.

The contest was fierce but short. Nothing could withstand our onslaught. The Cavaliers gave way, and, escaping across the island, made for their boats, reaching which they crossed over to St. Mary's, leaving us in possession of their cannon, muskets, and pikes, and pistols, besides several prisoners.

A lodgment on the island being thus effected, we threw up trenches to prevent our position being retaken when night closed down upon us. We had to keep a strict watch, the men sleeping with their arms by their sides, for at any moment we might be attacked. When morning came, the admiral, with a reinforcement, landed, and immediately gave the word to advance. We passed over a high ridge which crossed the island, and descended on the other side, when a view broke on our sight which for picturesque beauty could scarcely be surpassed.

Before us rose St. Mary's Island, with its castle and ramparts; below, in the centre of the roadstead, lay the war ships of the Cavaliers, with the prizes they had captured, the blue expanse bordered by jutting points and fantastic rocks of various shapes, while the surrounding shores were covered with umbrageous trees, green fields, and rich orchards.

The admiral at once selected a point overlooking the harbour and roadstead, on which he forthwith ordered a battery to be erected.

No sooner were the works thrown up than we opened a hot fire on the castle and other fortifications, as well as on the vessels, which, cutting their cables, endeavoured to escape up various channels hitherto concealed from our sight.

The admiral, however, no sooner seeing that, at the distance we were from the castle, our shot could produce but little effect on it, returned on board, leaving Captain Morris to continue the siege, and ordering his nephew and me to follow.

We now found that he had devised a new plan of attack. Summoning all the lighter frigates, he placed on board a

number of men, and supplied each also with several guns of
larger calibre than they were wont to carry. Going himself
on board one of them, the *Fox*, with Robert Blake, Lancelot
and I, he led the way towards a narrow channel between
the open sea and the roadstead, directly opposite St. Mary's.

Our progress was slow, but by dint of towing and
warping we advanced unmolested, until we reached the
harbour of St. Mary's.

The castle, as we were seen approaching, commenced
firing, when dropping our anchors, with springs to our
cables, we returned the salute with our broadsides.

In a few minutes the harbour, which had looked so
bright and calm, was canopied by dense wreaths of smoke ;
the shot came crashing into the sides of the vessels, or
splashing into the water, while our ears were deafened by
the roar of the guns thundering from the castle and from
our own and the corsairs' fleets.

Though frequently struck, we received less damage
than I had anticipated, while we soon perceived that the
ill-constructed walls of the castle and fortifications were
crumbling away from the effect of our shot.

Night coming on put an end to the attack, and we
retired out of range of the enemy's guns. But our
admiral had no intention of desisting.

All night long we remained at our quarters, thinking it
possible that the enemy might venture to board us in
their boats during the darkness. More than once an
alarm was raised and the men flew to their guns, but the
night passed off tranquilly ; the Cavaliers had no stomach
for such an enterprise. Morning broke at last. The
castle walls, wearing a battered appearance, rose above
the calm water shining in the rays of the rising sun ; the
air was soft and balmy, a thin haze softening the more
rugged features of nature.

Prayers being offered up, and breakfast over, we stood in to our former position to recommence our work of the previous day.

Forthwith the guns on both sides began blazing away. "Hurrah!" cried Lancelot, "we shall soon bring matters to a conclusion. Look there!" Turning my eyes in the direction he pointed, I saw that our fire concentrated on one side of the fortress was producing a considerable effect. Huge pieces of masonry, earth, and stones came toppling over and slipping into the ditch, and ere long we perceived that our shot had produced a practicable breach, through which our troops would quickly effect an entrance.

The admiral then ordered them to prepare for the assault, but as they were advancing, a flag of truce was thrown out from the walls, and a herald descending came off in a boat to the ship with a message from Sir John, requesting to hold a parley.

It was agreed to, when conditions were proposed. Sir John offered, provided that the lives of the officers and men were spared, to surrender the islands with their garrisons, stores, arms, ammunition, standards, and all implements and materials of war; the soldiers and seamen being allowed to enter the nation's service, while the gentlemen were to be sent to London, to await the decision of Parliament.

To these terms, which were considered very favourable to the Royalists, the admiral consented, and Sir John, with his corsair companions, were put on board Admiral Askew's squadron to be carried to Plymouth.

We, in the meantime, were employed in collecting the various vessels which had been captured by the pirates and bringing them under our guns, lest some of the rovers might attempt to get off and pursue their old calling in other regions. Lancelot and I were employed in this service. We had boarded several when we caught sight over the land of the masts of another moving slowly through the water; we gave chase, and soon came up with her. The captain vowed that he had no intention of escaping, but appearances were against him. On getting back to the harbour, we sent him on board the flag-ship to answer for his conduct.

While we were on board we entered into conversation with an intelligent fellow, Ned Watkins by name, who acted as boatswain. He seemed to be fond of making use of his tongue. Lancelot, wishing to ascertain something about the corsair career of these ships, asked him if his vessel, the *Speedwell*, had been long at sea and what prizes she had taken.

"Never craft had worse luck," he answered. "We had sailed from Jersey with the *Hector*, another ship of the same size as ours, carrying eighty men and twenty guns, bound out to Lisbon, or anywhere, as long as we could fall in with that royal rover, Prince Rupert, when, as we were coming down Channel, a strong gale blowing, we sighted a hoy, a tight little hooker, somewhere off the Start. We both made chase, for a small fish is better than no fish at all, and soon came up with her, though she tried her best to escape. The *Hector*, which boarded her, took out her people and several passengers, for so I judged them to be, as they wore petticoats, and all her cargo, and then a crew being put on board the prize we made sail for Scilly, where we had been ordered to call on our way southward. A strong north-westerly gale, however, which caught us just as we neared the islands, drove us out to sea, and when it moderated and we were about to beat back, seven large ships hove in sight, which, as they approached, we saw carried the Parliamentary flag. As we had no wish to fall into their hands, we made sail to escape, and succeeded in keeping ahead of them, but during the night we lost sight of the *Hector*. In what direction she was steering we could not make out. When morning dawned, however, we caught a glimpse of the enemy's squadron, and from the way they were steering, we had little doubt that they were in pursuit of her. By furling all sail we escaped observation, and three days afterwards managed to get back with the sloop to Scilly."

" What became of the *Hector?* " I inquired eagerly, at once feeling certain that the vessel she had captured was the hoy in which Mr. Kerridge and his party were proceeding to Plymouth.

" From that day to this I have heard nothing of her," answered the boatswain. " My idea is, if she escaped from the Roundhead squadron, and not managing to get into the Tagus, that she ran up the Straits to do some privateering on her own account. Her commander, Captain Kerby, was not a man to let a chance escape him, and he had been in charge of a trader to all parts of the Mediterranean."

We questioned and cross-questioned Ned Watkins, but he could give us no further information. Lancelot and I talked the subject over.

" My father and our sisters were not drowned, then, as some suppose, and may still be alive, though held, I fear, in durance, or they would have found means of communicating with us," he said. " That the *Hector* did not reach the Tagus we may be pretty certain, for if she had, my father would have contrived to send a message to the admiral. If Watkins is right in his conjectures, she must then have gone up the Straits, and she may or may not have afterwards joined the Prince's squadron, though I am inclined to think she did not, or we should have heard of her from the prizes we took, and she was certainly not among the vessels we destroyed. It follows then that she met with some other fate."

"Alack! and that may be a disastrous one," I exclaimed. "Too probably we shall never again hear of the dear ones."

"Not if we don't search for them," answered Lancelot "but I have an idea. What do you say to obtaining leave from the admiral to fit out one of the vessels we have just taken, and to go and look for them? We may learn where the *Hector* has been, and by that means trace them. I cannot bring myself to believe that they are lost."

I fully entered into Lancelot's plan, which we speedily matured. He at once went to Robert Blake, who, approving of our proposal, undertook to speak to his uncle.

Before long the admiral sent for us. "I can ill spare any trustworthy officers, but your cause is a sacred one, and you shall have the best vessel you can find, with such men among the prisoners as will volunteer, and whom you deem fitted for the service. I will undertake to pay their wages and all other expenses, and you may gain such information of what is going on in the Mediterranean as may be of use to our country."

We heartily thanked the admiral, and taking our leave, hastened to carry out our intentions.

We soon, with Lieutenant Blake's assistance, fixed on a vessel, appropriately called the *Good Hope*. She was in seaworthy condition, with stores of all sorts on board, and carried twenty guns. Her complement of men we had no difficulty in obtaining, as the corsairs who had just been captured were glad to obtain good pay and to escape having to serve on board the Parliamentary ships.

Lancelot was appointed captain, I went as his first lieutenant, and Dick, who got leave from the admiral, as

his second, while Martin Shobbrok went as gunner, and
Ned Watkins volunteered to act as boatswain.

Getting such further stores, provisions, arms, and ammunition on board as we required for a long cruise, we bade
our friends "Good-bye," and making sail stood away from
the Scilly Islands, which we soon ran out of sight.

CHAPTER VIII.

CLOSE QUARTERS.

HE *Good Hope* had got well to the southward. Hitherto things had gone on smoothly, though we found our crew less inclined to submit to discipline than we desired. Neither did Martin and Watkins pull very amicably together.

At first we thought that the old gunner was inclined to demand more respect from the boatswain than the latter was inclined to pay, but one night, while I was keeping watch on deck, Martin came up to me. He looked round to ascertain that no one was near, as if he had something of importance to communicate.

"Well, old friend, what has happened?" I asked.

"Nothing as yet, but something will happen, if we don't look sharp," he answered. "I mistrust that fellow Watkins."

"That's just what I wanted to speak to you about. It would be better for the discipline of the ship if you could make friends with him. Unless the officers pull together, we cannot hope to keep a crew like ours in order."

I

" It's not my fault that we have disputes," answered the old man ; " he's always trying to pick a quarrel with me, and to bring me into disrepute with the crew.   I have had my eye on him of late, and I have observed that he is constantly going among the men when below, talking to them in the most familiar way, endeavouring to make them think him a very fine fellow, to gain them over to some plan or other he has in his head."

I questioned Martin, thinking he must have been deceived, but he was positive that he had not.

" I will tell the captain what you say, and I'll take such precautions as are possible," I replied.   " In the meantime let me know what men are likely to hold staunch to us if your surmises should prove correct."

" I think I can find a dozen God-fearing men, who were compelled against their will to serve with the Malignants. The rest are a drunken, rollicking, swearing lot, who would be ready to carry out any evil deed Watkins may propose."

" With a dozen good men and ourselves, being prepared beforehand, we may be able to counteract any plan the boatswain has in view," I observed.   " Do you, Martin, secure those who you think you can trust, and I will consult with the captain as to the precautions which may be necessary.   Go below, now, and take care no one discovers that we suspect Watkins."

As soon as Dick came on deck, I told him what Martin had said, and he promised to be on the alert ; then going below, I went into Lancelot's cabin, and we held a consultation together on the subject.   He at once arrived at the conclusion that Watkins had conceived the possibility of taking the ship from us, and, should he succeed, that he intended to join Prince Rupert, or make a piratical cruise on his own account.

He might hope, by hoisting the Prince's flag, to be taken for one of his squadron, and be able to sell his prizes in a Spanish or French port, or if he could not, by running across to the West Indies to dispose of them there. As Martin did not lead us to suppose that Watkins' plans were mature, we agreed that we might wait without apprehensions of mutiny for a day or two, or perhaps longer, until we ascertained who were the men we could trust.

Next morning a heavy gale sprang up, and the crew had plenty of work in shortening sail and attending to their other duties, so that they had little time for plotting, were they so inclined. The gale lasted three days, the sea running mountains high, and threatening to engulph the ship. During the time we marked the way the men performed their duties, and noted such as appeared the best seamen, believing that those generally would prove the most trustworthy. When the storm was over the ship was put on her proper course and all sail made, for we were eager to get through the Straits to prosecute the object of our voyage.

We were now about the latitude of Cadiz. Dick Harvey was on deck, I was seated in the cabin with Lancelot, when Martin came in under pretence that he had been sent for to receive orders.

"I was not mistaken in my suspicions, Captain Kerridge," he said. "Watkins has won over well-nigh two-thirds of the crew, and their intention is as soon as they get inside the Straits to seize the ship and join Prince Rupert, if he is still up the Mediterranean, and if not, to follow him wherever he has gone, making prizes of all the craft they can fall in with, to supply themselves with provisions and stores. They have learned a pretty lesson from their Cavalier leaders, and it is natural that they should desire to follow it."

" But have you found any men on whom you can rely?"
asked Lancelot.

" That's just what I was going to tell you I have done,"
answered the old gunner. "There are twelve I have
spoken to who have promised to fight to the last, rather
than let their shipmates follow such desperate courses, and
there are six others who are not likely to join the mutineers
when they find there is a party to oppose them. It has been
so ordered by Providence that I have discovered a young
nephew of mine, who, having been seemingly won over by
Watkins, is in all his secrets. When he found out who I
was, he told me everything, believing that to do so was for
the good of us all. I advised him not to let it be known
that he had changed sides. He is a sharp lad, and though
he has been in bad company, he has not forgotten the
lessons his mother taught him, and wishes to do what
is right. Thus I am kept informed of all the purposes of
the mutineers, who are not likely to take us by surprise,
as they have not yet secured any of the arms."

We settled, to prevent them from doing so, to lock up
all the small arms and ammunition in one of the after cabins,
without allowing the crew to know what we had done.
Lancelot then directed Martin to go forward, as he wished
not to excite suspicion by keeping him in the cabin longer
than was necessary. We at once armed ourselves, and
either Martin, Lancelot, Dick, or I kept watch on deck,
while we took care always to have two trustworthy men at
the helm.

Martin assured us that the mutineers had no suspicion
that their designs were known. The weather had again
become fine, and we ran through the Straits of Gibraltar.
The moment the mutineers proposed to execute their plan
was approaching. Martin brought us word that they
intended to seize the ship at midnight, putting in irons all

who refused to join them, and to kill us should any resistance be offered.

As soon as it was dark, we ran two of the guns called "murtherers" through the ports of the after castle opening on the main deck, which should an enemy when boarding gain a footing there, are intended to rake it.

We also loaded and placed in readiness arms for about a score of men, who we hoped would side with us, while we also barricaded all the doors which led to the after part of the ship.

When all was ready, Martin, going below, told the men he could trust to muster aft.

One by one they crept up, so as not to attract the attention of the rest. As they came up we put arms into their hands, and stationed them under the after castle. To our satisfaction we found that we had as many as we had expected, who all swore to protect us with their lives from the mutineers.

Before the expected moment all our arrangements had been made. The sea was calm, a gentle breeze filled the sails, and the ship glided on, leaving a long trail of bright light astern.

Midnight came, when the captain's voice was heard, summoning all hands on deck to shorten sail. The crew, supposing that the ship was about to be struck by one of those white squalls which sometimes come on with fearful suddenness in the Mediterranean and lay over many a stout ship, hurried up from below, and instinctively sprang aloft. The boatswain having remained on deck, Dick and I, with two men we called to our aid, rushed forward, and seizing him dragged him aft.

This being done, the captain shouted—

"The squall will not strike us, lads; let fall the canvas and haul aft the sheets."

The crew, ignorant of what had occurred, obeyed, and were then ordered on deck. There they stood waiting for the signal the boatswain was to give them to set on us. There were three other ringleaders. The captain called two of them aft by name to take the helm. They came without hesitation, supposing that it would afford them a better opportunity for carrying out their plan. Instantly they were seized and placed in irons, the darkness greatly favouring our proceedings, as the rest of the crew could not see what was taking place. The third man, fortunately for us, coming aft was recognised by Martin, who, seizing him, we had him in limbo before he could be rescued.

The crew not finding the signal they expected given, crowded together, calling to their ringleaders and to each other.

Some among them now suspecting what had occurred, cried out that they were betrayed, and summoning the rest to the rescue, they advanced towards the place where their companions were confined.

On they came, armed with handspikes, belaying pins, boat stretchers, knives and axes, the only weapons they could procure, with threatening gestures, well able, it seemed, to overwhelm us.

"Stay where you are," shouted Lancelot; "the guns are loaded. If you advance a step further we fire. You know the consequences."

The mutineers, well aware that the guns would sweep the decks and hurl them in a moment into eternity, stopped short. Not one of them ventured to utter a word.

"My lads," continued their young captain, "you have been deceived by artful men, who would have led you to your destruction. I have no desire to injure one of you, and will overlook your conduct if you return to your duty. You engaged with me and my friends for a worthy cause, to search for some helpless ladies and an old man who are perchance held in bondage by the enemies of our country. We trusted to you as honest Englishmen to fulfil your engagements. Let it not be said that you turned renegades to a noble cause. Some of you have sisters and parents for whom you would be ready to fight. Are you then acting like brave men by turning against your officers? I will not believe that you are so base and worthless. Now, lads, let me see who will stand by us. Those who would keep to their pledges come over to starboard, while the rest stand on the larboard side."

For a short time the men hesitated, then first one, then another, and finally the whole body came over to the starboard side.

"I thought it would be so!" exclaimed the captain. "Thank you, lads. I intend to trust you; and if we meet an enemy, I am sure you will prove that you are true British seamen."

The crew gave a hearty cheer in reply, and that cheer must have proved to the leaders of the mutiny that their influence over the men was lost.

To prevent them committing further mischief, we kept them in irons, intending to deliver them over to the first English ship of war we should meet.

Next morning, from the way the men behaved, and the quietness which prevailed, no one would have supposed that a fearful conflict had been imminent the previous night. They, indeed, went about their regular duties with more than usual alacrity. We let them see, however, that we were prepared, should they be inclined for mischief.

Our intention was to visit Sardinia, Majorca, Minorca, and other islands in that direction, then to run down the coast of Italy and Sicily, and afterwards steer for the Levant, making inquiries at all places and of all the vessels

we met for the missing *Hector*. We were many weeks thus
employed, often being delayed by calms and kept long in
port while prosecuting our inquiries.

When off Elba we sighted several ships showing English
colours. We ran down to them, and found that they formed
part of a squadron under Commodore Bodley. Heaving to,
we lowered a boat, and I took Master Watkins with the
three other prisoners on board the commodore's ship, telling
him of the trick they wished to play us.

" They'll not attempt a like one again," answered the
commodore. " We shall probably engage with the enemy
before long, and they will then have an opportunity of
retrieving their characters."

. As the calm came on, I was able to visit each ship and
make inquiries for the *Hector;* but no tidings could I gain
of her.

It would occupy too much space were I to describe the
places we visited, and all the adventures we met with.

We lay for several days in the beautiful Bay of Naples
to refit, and then stood across for Sicily, where we saw
Mount Etna casting up fire and smoke, and afterwards
coming off the island of Stromboli, we were well nigh over-
whelmed by the showers of ashes which fell on our deck,
making the men believe that we were about to be over-
whelmed, or that the day of judgment had come. Fellows
who had never before prayed, fell down on their knees and
cried for mercy.

A breeze springing up, we got once more under the blue
sky, and they quickly forgot their fears. Hitherto we had
been sadly disappointed. Had the *Hector* touched at any
of the ports we had visited she would have been remembered, as she was, as Watkins had described her, a stout
ship of peculiar build. We should have regretted losing
him, as he might have been able to identify her, had not

two of the men who remained served on board her, and
they declared that should they set eyes on the old *Hector*,
they should know her among a hundred such craft. We
resolved, at all events, to continue our search as long as we
had the means of procuring provisions and stores. We had
no small difficulty, however, in keeping our unruly crew in
order ; accustomed as most of them had been to the corsair
life, they longed for the excitement of the battle and chase,
and murmured at the peaceable work in which we were engaged. We promised them, therefore, that they should
have fighting enough should we fall in with an enemy to
our country, and of such England had many by this time,
Dutch, French and Spaniards, though the Italian princes
and Portuguese wisely wished to keep on friendly terms.

We had got some distance to the eastward of Malta, when
a calm came on, and we lay with our canvas flapping
against the masts, the sea shining like glass, and not a
cloud overhead to dim the blue heavens or to shield our
heads from the rays of the burning sun. The crew lay
about the decks overcome by the heat, and grumbling at the
idle life to which they were doomed. The red sun went
down, and the pale moon rose, casting a silvery light over
the slumbering ocean. Not a ripple broke the mirror-like
surface of the deep.

" We must give these fellows something to do, or they'll
be brewing mischief," observed Lancelot, as we listened to
the growling tones which came from forward.

" Unless we turn corsairs, or fall in with a Hollander or
a Don, I do not see what we can give them to do," answered
Dick.

" The chances are we shall not have long to wait, or we
may encounter a storm. That will give them some occupation, especially if it carries away some of our spars," I
observed, laughing.

We were in truth put to our wits' end to keep our men in good temper. Again the sun rose, and from the appearance of the sky there appeared every probability that the calm would continue. We immediately set the men to work with paint brushes and tar brushes, made them scrub the decks, and black down the rigging. We then exercised them at the guns. They were thus employed when, looking to the southward, I caught sight of a white sail rising above the horizon.

" She can't move without wind, and if so, she'll be bringing up a breeze," observed Dick. " We shall soon be throwing the spray over our bows as we make way again through the water."

Still the ship lay as immovable as before, her masts and spars, her black rigging, her white sails and shining hull reflected on the glass-like surface ; at the same time the stranger got closer and closer, and now her topsails appeared, next her courses.

" She's a big craft, that ; twice the size of the *Good Hope*, I opine," observed Martin. " If she's a friend, she may bring us news, but if she's an enemy we shall have to up stick and run for it."

· " Not until we see how many teeth she carries," said the captain, who overheard the remark. " Big as she is, the *Good Hope* may be able to tackle her."

While we were speaking, our loftier canvas began to swell and flutter, then the topsails and courses flapped against the masts, and cat's-paws ran playfully over the water. Presently ripples were seen on all sides, and every sail swelled out. The ship gathered way, but instead of keeping before the wind, the captain ordered the maintopsail to be backed, and we lay to waiting for the stranger, while our white flag with a red cross was run up to the peak. Hardly had it blown out than the approaching ship showed her colours, and the design of a crescent moon proved that she was Turkish, or belonged to Tunis, Tripoli, or some other of the Barbary States.

"My lads," cried Lancelot, "we shall probably have to fight yonder ship if she proves what I suppose her to be. If we capture her we shall obtain a rich prize. If she takes us, we shall have our throats cut, or be carried into slavery."

"We will fight her, and beat her," cried the men, and they gave utterance to a loud cheer.

"Brace round the main-yard, then," cried the captain, and the ship stood on close-hauled, ready to tack, so that if possible we might gain the weather-gauge. The stranger seeing this altered her course, in order to prevent our doing what we proposed. At length, finding that we could not gain the advantage we wished, we ran under her lee, and Lancelot in a loud tone ordered her to strike to the Commonwealth of England.

As a haughty refusal was the answer, we opened fire, hoping to knock away a mast or some of her spars, and thus be able to gain the position we desired; but the corsair, for such the stranger undoubtedly was, replied with a broadside of upwards of twenty guns, the shot from which passing between our masts, did no further damage than cutting away some of our running rigging.

We now stood on yard-arm to yard-arm, firing our guns as rapidly as they could be run in and loaded. Our enemies meantime were not idle, and their shot came crashing pretty thickly on board. Two of our men were killed and others wounded. But we judged that we were committing more damage than we received. Many of our shots went through and through the corsair's sides, others swept her decks and killed several of her crew. Still, from her superior size and greater number of guns, it was

probable before we could take her that she might so
seriously damage our little frigate that we might be
prevented from prosecuting our object.

Notwithstanding this, Lancelot had no idea of retreating
from the fight, and it only made him more anxious to gain
a speedy victory. It was soon seen that the corsair was
suffering the most in her hull, though her masts and spars
had hitherto escaped. On the other hand, we had lost our
fore-topmast, and shortly afterwards our fore-yard came
down by the run on deck, killing two of our men. Still
these disasters did not induce us to relax our efforts.

Our crew, now that they were put on their mettle, showed
that they were sturdy Englishmen, and as our shot went
crashing through the side of our big opponent they cheered
again and again, believing that she would soon be compelled to strike.

Lancelot stood on the after castle, watching every move-
ment of the enemy. At last his voice shouted, " Boarders!
be prepared to repel boarders!" and as he spoke the big
ship was seen bearing down, evidently intending to run
alongside. Our men had hangers and pistols in their belts.
Those not required to work the guns seized the boarding
pikes and stood ready to spring to that part of the ship's
side where the enemy might board us.

The corsair glided up, and her bow striking ours, she
hooked on to our fore-chains. The next instant a countless
number of swarthy figures with turbaned heads, bright
cimeters flashing in their hands, swarmed in the rigging of
the corsair and came leaping down on our deck

Led by Lancelot, Dick and I fighting by his side, we
met them with hanger, pike, and pistol, driving them back
over the bulwarks, or cleaving them from head to chine as
they got within reach of our swords.

Those who were about to follow, seeing the rate of the

PREPARED TO REPEL BOARDERS.

first, held back, and the next moment the ships separated.
Ere they did so their sides were brought close to each other,
and I saw a man make a tremendous spring from that of
the enemy and grip hold of our bulwarks, to which he
clung desperately, crying out—

"I am an Englishman; save me, save me!" Several
shots were fired at him by the corsairs; but he escaped,
and some of our men rushing to his rescue hauled him on
board.

"To the guns, to the guns!" shouted Lancelot, and
we again began to work our artillery with the same rapidity
as before.

CHAPTER IX.

THE CORSAIR BEATEN OFF.

FTER the failure of her attempt to board us, the corsair hauled aft her sheets and shot ahead of the *Good Hope*. We believing that she intended to rake us, quickly got head-sail on the ship, and by squaring away the after-yards, and brailing up the mizen, put her before the wind, all the time blazing away as fast as we could with our guns. Instead, however, of passing either astern or ahead of us, which having all her canvas set, she might easily have done, the corsair kept on a wind, and presently, when beyond the range of our guns, going about she stood away to the south-west. We had beaten off our big assailant, and we might possibly in a longer contest have compelled her to strike or sent her to the bottom, but we were in no condition to follow her. All hands being required to repair damages, some time passed before we could question the stranger who had taken refuge on board us. As he looked sick and careworn, Lancelot had directed that he should be conducted to the cabin, where, the ship having at length been put somewhat to rights, I was and hurl her, a helpless wreck, on the rocky coast. A few other captains imitated the example of their dauntless commander, but it was impossible to remain in sight of Kinsale. At length, the weather moderating, we once more came off the old headland, and, by degrees the ships assembling, the frigates were sent in towards the harbour's mouth to inspect the squadron of Prince Rupert. They returned with the intelligence that the corsair prince, with several of his ships, had escaped, leaving behind, however, a considerable number, which fell into our hands.

CHAPTER VI.

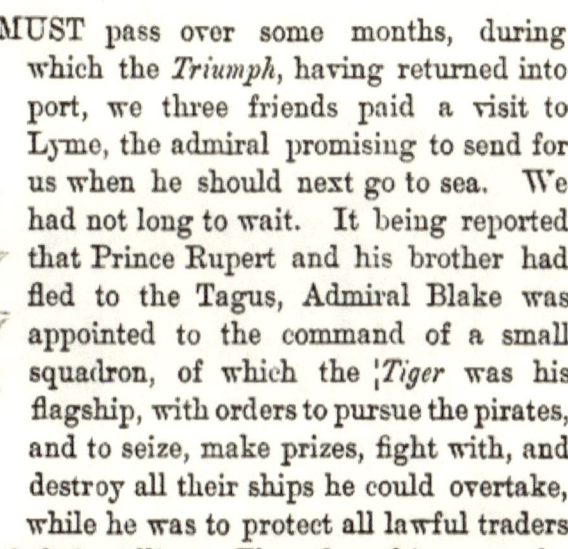

MUST pass over some months, during which the *Triumph*, having returned into port, we three friends paid a visit to Lyme, the admiral promising to send for us when he should next go to sea. We had not long to wait. It being reported that Prince Rupert and his brother had fled to the Tagus, Admiral Blake was appointed to the command of a small squadron, of which the ¦*Tiger* was his flagship, with orders to pursue the pirates, and to seize, make prizes, fight with, and destroy all their ships he could overtake, while he was to protect all lawful traders in the exercise of their calling. The other ships were the , *Tenth*, *Whelp*, *Sigent*, and *Constant Warwick*, carrying altogether one hundred and fourteen guns.

We were glad to find that young Robert Blake was one of the lieutenants of the *Tiger*, and equally rejoiced were we to see Martin Shobbrok walking the deck with a chain and silver whistle round his neck doing duty as boatswain. Although it was midwinter, no time was lost, and with a fair breeze we stood down channel. The winds, and the necessity of chasing every suspicious sail, prevented us

ADMIRAL BLAKE'S SQUADRON.

from reaching our destination—the mouth of the Tagus—until the approach of spring. To our infinite satisfaction, we found that the Prince's squadron was at anchor in the river, and forthwith the admiral despatched his nephew, whom I had the honour of accompanying, with a message to King John of Portugal, requesting permission to attack the ships of Prince Rupert, belonging to the Commonwealth of England, and carried off by treachery. I had never before been in a king's palace ; I have not the power, however, to describe the finely dressed ladies and gentlemen we saw, or the forms and ceremonies we went through. The king, or rather one of his ministers—who spoke for him—declared that he could permit no such proceeding, that the princes were his guests, and that we must take our departure without injuring them.

" The king sends us back, as he thinks, with a flea in our ears, but it is a flea which will tickle his majesty before long," observed Lieutenant Blake, who had something of his uncle's humour.

We returned on board the *Tiger*, and reported the result of our mission, when the admiral immediately ordered a squadron of boats to enter the river. I went in one of them. As we approached a white stone castle shining brightly in the sun, near the mouth, a puff of smoke issued from one of the embrasures. Another and another followed, the shot splashing into the water close to us.

On this the commander of the expedition, according to the orders received, returned to the squadron.

The admiral, curling his whiskers, sent to the castle to inquire why his boats had been stopped. The officer replied that his orders were to prevent any foreign ships sailing up the river. The admiral on this despatched another embassy to King John, demanding the reason for his conduct, but received as unsatisfactory a reply as before. The Portuguese king was not aware with whom he had to deal, and fancied that Blake would sail away without taking further notice of the affair.

In spite of the threats of the governor of Belim Castle, the *Tiger* leading the way, the squadron sailed into the river, not a shot being fired at us, and we brought up in Viera Bay.

Here some weeks passed, the crews fuming at the delay, and hoping every day that we might be able to get at the corsairs and punish them as they deserved. Our men were frequently on shore, when they constantly met the sailors of the Prince's squadron, on friendly terms.

Occasionally, however, there were quarrels, when our men jeered at the others, calling them pirates and robbers, and expressing a wonder that they should be willing to serve under such leaders as Rupert and his brother. Others of our people acted more wisely, and succeeded in inducing a considerable number of the Prince's men to desert and come on board our ships. This greatly enraged the Prince, who strung up several poor fellows found making their way to us. Still, others came off, and one of them told us that the *Swallow*, a ship of thirty-six guns, had actually got under weigh and was on the point of escaping, when the intention of her officers and crew being discovered, she was brought back. Some time after this, three boats under command of Lieutenant Blake were sent on shore to fill our casks at the fountain where we usually obtained water; Lancelot and I accompanied him. As there was no fear of our men deserting, we allowed some of those not required for the work in hand to stroll a short distance inland, Lieutenant Blake going with them, while I remained to superintend the watering party.

I was thus engaged when I heard some shots fired, and saw Lancelot, who had gone a little way off, running towards me.

" What's the matter?" I inquired.

"Our shipmates have been attacked by a party of Cavaliers and Portuguese hidalgoes, who have, I fear, got hold of Lieutenant Blake. If we bring up the men quickly, we may rescue him before he is carried off," he answered.

Calling our people together, some of whom were rolling the casks down to the boats, Lancelot and I led them in the direction we had heard the shots. We had not gone far when we caught sight of our party warmly engaged with a number of persons in hunting dresses, some being English, others Portuguese, among whom we distinguished our lieutenant, held by two Portuguese, while others were pointing their swords at his breast. Almost before they discovered us, uttering a loud shout we were upon them. The lieutenant on seeing us, shaking off the grasp of the two men who held him, knocked up the blade of another, and seizing the sword of a fourth, sprang towards us. At that moment, however, a strong reinforcement arriving we had to retreat, with our faces to the foe. Several of our men fell dead, and others were wounded. An attack also was made on six of our people who had been separated from us, when, with the exception of one who cut his way out from among those surrounding the party, the rest were made prisoners. We showed so bold a front that, notwithstanding our heavy losses, the Cavaliers and their allies did not venture to follow us, though they fired a volley which killed one more of our men and wounded another. We at length reached the boats, and taking the casks on board, pulled away to communicate the circumstance to the admiral. Lieutenant Blake told him that he had recognised Prince Maurice as well as two or three of his officers, and that the other leaders of our assailants were Portuguese grandees.

The admiral was highly indignant, but how to punish

our dastardly foes as they deserved was a difficult matter
to determine. The King of Portugal would certainly refuse
to deliver up the offenders, and we were not as yet in a
position to compel him.

We had therefore to bide our time.

That evening, as I was walking the deck with Lancelot,
we saw a small boat coming off from the shore. She had
but one man in her. He hailed as he got alongside, and
asked if he might be permitted to come on board, as he had
a communication to make to the admiral.

Permission was at once given, and after remaining a
short time in the cabin, the stranger took his departure,
when the admiral came on deck and ordered the ports to be
closed.

Soon after this another boat was seen coming off, containing a person dressed as a Portuguese tradesman, and
rowed by two negroes. The boat also carried a large cask.
After coming up under the stern, she pulled round on the
starboard side. The seeming Portuguese then handed up
a letter, which one of the officers took. It purported to
come from a merchant on shore, stating that he had sent
off a cask of oil for the use of the crew. The white man
was still seated in the boat, when the boatswain and two
other men came aft and informed the admiral that they
were very sure he was no Portuguese, but one of the persons belonging to Prince Rupert's ship whom they frequently
met on shore.

"Let the cask remain in the boat, and order the man up
the side," said the admiral.

The Portuguese, on receiving the order, showed a great
disinclination to obey, and said something to the negroes,
who were getting out their oars to shove off when three of
our men jumped into the boat, and having secured her, the
white man and two blacks were brought on deck. The

admiral now turning to the boatswain ordered him to reeve a rope to the yard-arm.

"So my friend," he said, turning to the white prisoner, "you intended to blow up this ship and all on board. If that cask is full of oil my information is incorrect, but if not, be prepared for the consequences."

On this the man fell on his knees, and pleading for mercy, offered to reveal the plot he had been engaged to carry out.

"You deserve death, but your life shall be spared if you speak the truth," said the admiral.

The man then confessed that he had been employed by the Cavaliers to destroy the admiral and his flag-ship; that the cask was double-headed, and that the interior was filled with gunpowder and missiles of all sorts; that between the two heads there was a lock so contrived that on being opened it would fire a quick match and cause the whole to explode.

"As you understand its mechanism, you shall be employed in extracting its contents," said the admiral.

The man on hearing this looked greatly disconcerted, but was forced to obey. The carpenter having provided him with tools, he descended into the boat, when she was towed some distance from the ship, where she was anchored, and the oars being removed, he was left to operate alone on the cask.

He was watched with great interest as he cut a hole through the bottom. This done, he took out the contents and hove them overboard, when he hailed to say that the cask was empty.

The admiral then ordered him and the two blacks to depart with a message for the Prince, informing him of the miscarriage of his enterprise.

The Prince afterwards, we heard, spread a report that he and his brother, while out hunting, had been attacked by a party of men from Admiral Blake's fleet, and that he had in consequence allowed the attempt to be made to blow up the flag-ship. I should here say that on board the Prince's fleet were many Republicans, who sent the admiral information of all his intentions. We now heard that, fearing lest the King of Portugal should no longer be willing to afford him protection, Prince Rupert proposed putting to sea, and seeking his fortune in another direction.

On this, a calm coming on, our ships were towed down to the mouth of the river, where we lay ready to intercept him, and so the Prince's plan was defeated.

Some weeks went by, when Admiral Popham arrived with a strong reinforcement, and by one of the ships came letters to Lancelot and me, of which I will speak anon. The King of Portugal, just before this, throwing off all disguise, arrested several English merchants residing in Lisbon, and declared his intention of supporting the corsair princes.

No sooner was this news received on board our ships than the admiral sent word to the Portuguese government that he proposed to make reprisals. While the messenger was on the way, a number of ships were seen with all sails set coming out of the river. They proved to be richly laden merchantmen bound for the Brazils. As they approached, our squadron got under weigh, and before the Brazilian ships had time to retreat we surrounded them and captured the whole. As they were well armed, the officers and crews being removed, we sent all the men we could spare on board, and thus nine fine vessels were added to the strength of our fleet. Winter was approaching, and with it came heavy gales, greatly trying our ships. Information had been received that another richly laden fleet from the Brazils was expected in the river. We accordingly, our ships having been carefully fitted to encounter the fiercest storms, got under weigh and stood out to sea in order to watch for it. We had not long to wait, when one of the look-out frigates brought intelligence which made us all on the alert.

The commander stated that he had counted no less than twenty-three sail approaching under all the canvas they could carry.

On they came. The admiral ordered the signal to be thrown out to prepare for action. The Portuguese fleet approached, supposing our ships to be those of their own nation; and as far as we could judge, were in no way ready for battle. They advanced in gallant array, their admiral leading, but as they drew nearer their suspicions must have been aroused. They were soon convinced that we had hostile intentions, when the *Tiger*, standing across the bows of the flag-ship, ordered her to strike and heave to. A shot which struck us was the answer, when tacking so as to bring our other broadside to bear, we commenced firing away as fast as our guns could be run in and loaded.

The other ships imitated our example, each engaging one, and some two or three of the enemy. Again our commander ordered the Portuguese admiral to strike, but he refused, notwithstanding the fearful punishment we were inflicting on him. Our shots, fired at short range, were going through and through the sides between wind and water. Presently one of the enemy's ships astern of us was seen to be on fire. The flames spread rapidly, bursting out from her ports and climbing the tall masts. Another and another was speedily in the same predicament. The fate of these ships brought terror into the hearts of the enemy. Now the flag of a large ship attacked by the *Resolution* was hauled down. Now another struck, and quickly the antagonist of the *Constant Warwick* lowered her flag, allowing that gallant barque to pay her attentions to a second foe.

Cheer after cheer burst from the throats of our crew as they saw these rich prizes captured, while they redoubled the efforts they were making against the Portuguese flag-ship. Still the action continued raging in all directions over the blue ocean, canopied by a dark pall of smoke, which was increased each moment by the curling wreaths arising from the thundering guns. Every effort was now made by the Portuguese to escape, for their ships contained rich treasures which they were unwilling to lose, but their efforts were in vain. Like eager hounds heated by the chase, our ships, setting all sail, soon came up with the fugitives, whose masts and spars being knocked away, they hauled down their flag. Their admiral had been fighting long and bravely, when Martin Shobbrok, who was standing near me, exclaimed, pointing at her, "The Lord have mercy on their souls! Mark you not, Master Ben, how deep by the head is that stout Portugale ship? See, see! she is sinking lower and lower." Still the guns from her upper deck continued to belch forth flames and smoke. It seemed as if her crew were not aware of the fate awaiting them. Before another minute had elapsed shrieks and cries arose. Men were seen rushing up from below, and clambering on the bulwarks. Others were engaged in lowering the boats and throwing overboard planks and hen-coops, and pieces of furniture, and whatever they could lay their hands on.

"Cease firing!" cried our admiral, and not another shot was discharged at our helpless foe. Lower and lower sank the stout ship, her stern lifted high out of the water, then downwards she glided, her canvas set, her flag still flying, her commander and his officers still standing on the lofty after-castle, until that too disappeared beneath the wild waves which dashed over them, and soon even the main truck vanished beneath the surface, leaving a few struggling forms and pieces of wreck, and articles thrown overboard, floating on the spot she had lately occupied.

Stern necessity compelled us to sail in chase of her flying consorts, one of which proved to be the ship of the vice-admiral, who, taught a lesson by the fate of his chief, as we approached lowered his flag.

Seven of the smaller vessels which had sought safety at the commencement of the engagement in flight, being already close in with the mouth of the river, escaped, but we captured eleven large ships, not counting the admiral's which sank, and three others consumed by fire.

As soon as the prizes were secured, the boats were lowered to try and pick up any of the helpless people who might have escaped from the ships destroyed; but few only were rescued, though I am well assured that, had the admiral acted according to the dictates of his heart, he would rather have allowed the vice-admiral to escape than have delayed the attempt to save the perishing seamen.

As we could not enter the river, and another gale might come on, we lost no time in repairing damages and refitting the prizes, so that they might undertake the voyage to England.

Admiral Blake was well aware that the Portuguese would endeavour to revenge themselves for the loss they had suffered, but still undaunted, he prepared to resist their squadron, united to that of the Prince, should they venture to attack us.

Day after day we sailed backwards and forwards off the mouth of the river, or when a tempest threatened, shortening sail, we beat out to sea to avoid shipwreck, again to return the instant the wind moderated. This sort of work greatly added to the experience my companion and I had gained on the coast of Ireland, so that we could boast of being efficient seamen.

"You'll soon be made a lieutenant, Mr. Ben, and ere long a captain; and, when you get command of a ship, I hope that you'll apply to have me sent with you," said Martin to me one day as we were walking the deck together. "Although she may be only half the size of the *Tiger*, I would rather be with you than even with our good admiral, much as I love him. He is the man to win all hearts, not only because he is the best commander we ever had, but because he attends to the wants and looks after the interests of the men below him."

I promised Martin, if I lived to get the command of a ship, that I would obtain him as boatswain, should he not in the meantime be advanced to a higher grade such as his merits deserved.

"Martin Shobbrok is too old for a lieutenant, and besides, is no navigator, so that he would feel like a fish out of water," he answered. "He has been boatswain for the best part of his life, and boatswain he is willing to remain, unless he is made chief gunner, and no great learning is required for that."

Again we sighted the rock of Lisbon, when a thick mist came on, which shrouded it and the whole coast from sight. Notwithstanding the fog, a fresh breeze was blowing. We were steering on our usual course under easy sail, when, as I was on deck, with Martin pacing a short distance from me, he exclaimed—

"There's a tall ship close to us," and looking in the direction he pointed, I could dimly see through the fog a dark mass of canvas. The sound of the rattling and creaking of blocks, too, reached our ears.

"She's an enemy; to your guns, lads!" he shouted. "Go and tell the captain, Master Ben."

I ran aft to tell the commander, who, followed by the admiral, appeared on deck.

'Silence!'" he cried; "go to your quarters without beat of drum."

The guns were cast loose, and powder and shot brought from below, and our men stood ready for the next order. The phantom ship, for such she appeared, loomed larger and larger. The admiral divined her object—to run us on board.

"She's either the Portugale flag-ship or maybe that of Prince Rupert's himself," whispered Martin to me.

One thing was certain, that she was not one of our squadron. Silently she glided up under our lee.

"Now give it her, my lads," cried the admiral, and every gun from the starboard broadside was fired into the stranger.

Down came her fore-topmast by the run. Silence being no longer necessary, our crew gave a hearty cheer, hoping that we were about to tackle the stranger, but being under a press of sail, she shot past ahead, and so dense was the fog, that in a few seconds she had disappeared. We eagerly sought for her, but we searched in vain.

Next day, the fog having cleared away, the united fleets were discovered, but our admiral's object was to avoid a regular engagement, as no good could thereby be attained, and he contented himself with cutting off first one and then another of the enemy's ships.

"I know who tried to surprise us yesterday evening," exclaimed Martin. "The tall ship with the Prince's flag flying, and her fore-topmast gone, but she would have been surprised herself had she not slipped out of the way."

At length the admiral gained information that another large Brazilian fleet was at sea, which, being of far more value than the empty hulls of the Prince's squadron, we sailed in search of. After cruising about for several weeks, we heard that some of the Brazilian ships had

taken refuge in Spanish ports, and that others were at the
Azores. We accordingly sailed back to the Tagus.
Scarcely had we arrived than a frigate with a flag of truce
came to meet us, bringing intelligence that the corsair
princes had left the river, and that the king of Portugal
had sent an ambassador to England to sue for peace.

The admiral's work in the Tagus being accomplished, we
prepared for returning home. I mentioned that Lancelot
and Dick had received letters from Lyme. Lancelot's was
from his father's head factor, the other from Mr. Harvey.
They both gave us the same alarming intelligence which
affected Lancelot as well as me. They told us that Mr.
Kerridge and his daughter, accompanied by Audrey and
Mistress Margaret, her waiting-maid, had sailed in a hoy
bound for Plymouth, at which place, to their dismay, they
found she had not arrived. Some hours after leaving
Lyme, a heavy gale had arisen, but it was calculated that
the hoy might by that time have got into Plymouth,
or run back for Lyme, or found shelter in some other
harbour. Whether she had foundered, or run on the
Eddystone or on some other rock, or had been captured by
an enemy, no one could surmise, but that some sad
disaster had happened to her there could be no doubt.

The news of course caused Lancelot and me great grief,
in which our friend Dick heartily sympathised, as did
Lieutenant Blake, who had when at Lyme been well
acquainted with Mr. Kerridge and Cicely and my sweet
sister Audrey.

"Should the hoy have foundered, we must submit to
God's decrees; but should she, as is possible, have been
captured, we will, as soon as we are at liberty, search the
world over to discover the missing ones," he said, as he
wrung our hands, and told us how sincerely he entered
into our feelings.

able to join him. Finding that having been properly looked after and supplied with food he had much recovered, I inquired who he was and from whence he came.

"My name is Joseph Aylett; I am an Englishman and a sea officer," he answered. "I was captured many a long month ago, on board a vessel by a ship from Tunis, not far from where we now are. The night was dark, the sea smooth, a light breeze only filling our sails. Not a thought of danger entered our heads. A bad look-out must have been kept, for, without warning, suddenly a large ship ran us alongside before we could fly to our arms or fire a gun, and a whole host of Moors came swarming down on our decks. Resistance was useless, though had we been prepared we might have fought the enemy as you did and beaten her off. We were prisoners to the corsairs, and doomed, as we supposed, to a life-long slavery. If the lot of us men was hard, that of our female passengers was harder still. We had two poor young ladies with a waiting woman and their father, who had been taken on board against their will and compelled to accompany us out to these distant seas. Every respect had been shown to them by the captain and officers, of whom I was one, and we had promised to send them home by the first ship we should fall in with returning to England.

"As no blood had been shed we were better treated by the Moors than we had expected, the passengers even were allowed to remain in their cabins without molestation, and I was thankful to find that the young ladies did not make their appearance. Still I trembled to think to what indignities they might be exposed when carried on shore, and perhaps separated from each other and their father. Most of our crew were quickly removed to the corsair, their places being supplied by the Moors, but I and a few others were left on board to assist in working the ship.

K

A calm coming on prevented us from reaching Tunis for a couple of days. During the time, I turned in my mind the possibility of assisting the young ladies, and at length a plan occurred to me, by adopting which their position might be rendered less perilous than would otherwise be the case.

"We had had two young boys in the ship, son and nephew of the captain. The one had died from sickness, the other had fallen overboard and been drowned. Their clothes had been left in a chest, and when no one was looking, I possessed myself of the articles and carried them to their cabin. My object was quickly explained, and they at once expressed their willingness to follow my advice.

"Their father saw its wisdom, and leaving them to don the garments I had brought, I hastened away that I might not be perceived. Then telling the other officer left with me what I had done, we at once agreed as to the way we should behave to the seeming lads. We were, should we have an opportunity, to inform our captain, who was on board the corsair, of what we had done, and to treat them as if they were his son and nephew."

The feelings with which I listened to the officer's narrative can better be supposed than expressed. "Tell me, Mr. Aylett, who were those young ladies of whom you speak?" I asked, in an agitated voice.

"Their father was, I understand, a Roundhead, Kerridge by name, but otherwise a well-disposed, amiable gentleman whom I was glad to serve."

"Kerridge!" I exclaimed, not regarding his remark. "Tell me, sir, the name of the vessel on board which you were."

"The *Hector*," he replied.

All doubt vanished from my mind as to whom those unfortunate persons were.

"Go on, sir, I pray you," I said. "Tell me what happened next."

"The following morning, while we were some way off Tunis, the old gentleman accompanied by the two young ladies appeared on deck, but it would have required a keen eye to have discovered that they were not what they seemed. I forthwith went up to one of them and sang out, 'Lay hold of this rope and do as I do; now haul away.' The other joined us, and by the way the Moors looked at them, I felt satisfied that their disguise was not discovered.

"I then spoke to the old woman who attended on them, advising her to conceal their female attire.

"'I have taken good care of that, sir,' she answered. I've thrown some through a port and packed the rest in my chest; it won't be my fault if they are found out.'

"Our captors treated us with more civility than I had expected. I and the men left were doing our best to navigate the ship, and the Moors knew that we could not escape. No sooner, however, had we dropped anchor and furled sails in the harbour of Tunis, off the strong castle of Porto Ferino, than several boats came alongside, and we, as well as the poor passengers being mustered on deck, had our arms lashed behind us, by which treatment we knew that we were looked upon as slaves. We were then carried on shore to the slave market, where we found the rest of the crew of the *Hector*. I thought little of my own sufferings while reflecting on the sad fate to which Mr. Kerridge and his young companions were doomed. In a short time purchasers appeared, and the sale of the captives commenced. From the prices offered it was evident that the common men were looked upon as of greater value than the officers, from its being supposed that they were capable of performing more work.

"Most of the men had been disposed of, when an old Moor in magnificent costume, and several attendants, entered the bazaar. The prices of the men who remained, consisting of the boatswain and his mate, the gunner and three of his crew, all standing six feet high, with broad shoulders, had been considerably raised, but no bidders were forthcoming.

"I thought that the Moorish chief would have bought them, but on hearing the price named he turned away and pointed to Mr. Kerridge and the two boys. Satisfied with the sum asked, he at once paid it down, and they were transferred to the care of his black attendants. On seeing this the old woman rushed up to him, and by signs entreated that he would purchase her, amid much laughter, and finding that a very trifling amount was placed on her, he paid it over. I was thankful to find that the whole four were thus purchased by one master, and was wondering what would become of me, when the old Moor, looking into his purse, seemed to discover that he had sufficient for the purchase of another slave. After examining each of the officers, to my great satisfaction he fixed on me, for I had a fancy that he was likely to prove more kind-hearted than most of his countrymen, and that I might be of use to the young ladies and their father.

"Apparently well pleased with his purchases, the old Moor left the bazaar followed by his attendants, who led us along. Outside we found several camels, on which the whole party being mounted, we set off, following a road towards the interior. Although our chance of escape would be greatly lessened by being at a distance from the coast, I was thankful to get out of the town. At last we arrived at what looked like a large farm. It was the chief's residence, a number of smaller buildings surrounding it, and at the back large gardens, shaded by fine trees, with ponds and fountains and flower beds. The whole was under the care of a big black fellow, to whose charge Mr. Kerridge and I were committed. We found that it was intended we should labour in the garden, while the two seeming boys were destined to attend on the old chief, and Margaret on his wives and children. Our lot was thus happier than we could have expected, still there was the fear that the sex of the young ladies might be discovered, though, with Margaret's help, we hoped that this might be avoided. Of course, from the first Mr. Kerridge and I discussed the possibility of escaping, but, removed as we were from the coast, that we should succeed appeared almost impossible.

"I was one day labouring as usual, when the old chief came into the garden, accompanied by another person whom I recognised to be the captain of the ship which had captured us.

"He looked at me and inquired who I was. 'He is the man who brought the prize into the harbour,' he observed. 'I am in want of some good seamen for my new ship, and I will buy him of you, so name your price.'

"I was in hopes that the old chief would refuse, for though I might possibly, by getting on board ship effect my escape, yet I was unwilling to leave Mr. Kerridge and his daughters to their hard fate. I found, however, that the transfer had been made without the option of remaining being given me, so I was carried off by the captain, and in two days going on board the vessel he spoke of, I was ordered, under pain of having my brains blown out, to perform the duty of a lieutenant. As it would have been madness to resist, I tried to appear reconciled to my lot, though I resolved on the first opportunity to make my escape. It came sooner than I had expected.

"I confess when I sprang from the side of the corsair that I scarcely hoped to reach your deck alive."

I need not say into what a state of agitation Mr. Aylett's account threw me. He repeated it again when Lancelot and Dick came below, and it was with difficulty that we could attend to the duties of the ship, thinking of the means to be taken for rescuing those for whom we had searched so long. Mr. Aylett, however, gave us no hope of success. "It would be impossible even to communicate with them," he observed; "the only chance would be to send a message to their owner, and to offer a large sum for their ransom." How this message was to be sent was the question. Aylett pointed out that were he to go he should be immediately seized as a deserter and lose his life, while any other Englishman who might set foot in the country would be carried off to slavery.

Unfortunately, much time must elapse before even the best-formed plan could be put into execution, for so battered was our ship that it would be absolutely necessary to go into port and refit before we could venture on the coast.

It would be difficult to describe our feelings at the delay, yet our better judgment told us it must be endured. It was a satisfaction to know that Audrey and Cicely and Mr. Kerridge and poor Margaret were alive, and from Aylett's account not ill-treated; yet bondage in any form is hard to bear, and we could not tell what change for the worse in their circumstances might occur. Happily the weather remained calm, and enabled us to get up a fore-yard on which sail could be set, though we had no spar for a top-mast. The men worked with a will, for they feared that the Barbary corsair might return, and they had no wish to become slaves, which would be our lot should she succeed in capturing us.

A moderate breeze springing up from the southward, we were able to steer a course for Cagliari in the island of Sardinia, one of the few friendly ports in the Mediterranean, where we could refit and obtain provisions. We reached it without encountering an enemy, and lost no time in commencing the necessary repairs. Still we were in as much doubt as at first as to what means we should take to rescue our friends.

One thing was certain, that force would not avail. Should we reach the coast, our little ship would be blown out of the water by the Tunisian corsairs; or, should our whole crew land, we should be cut to pieces before we had advanced a mile into the country.

We talked of going on shore in disguise, but our ignorance of Arabic would betray us. Our only hope of success would be to negotiate, but the old Moor would probably demand a far higher ransom than we were able to pay, and very likely should we sail into the harbour, even with a flag of truce, the Moors would seize our vessel and help themselves to everything on board, while we should be carried off as slaves.

We had now been a long time without hearing from England, and were ignorant of the events taking place nearer home. Of one thing we felt certain, that Admiral Blake was not idle. If work was to be done, he was doing it.

The *Good Hope* was nearly ready for sea, but still our plan of proceeding was as unsettled as before, when a squadron of five ships with the flag of the Commonwealth flying was seen coming in from the southward. As soon as they had anchored, Lancelot and I went on board the flag-ship, to pay our respects to Commodore Bodley, the commander of the squadron, and to ask his advice and obtain his assistance in recovering our friends. We were

invited into his cabin, where we found several officers collected.   They were unanimous in the opinion that the
attempt to rescue Mr. Kerridge and his companions would
be madness without a strong force at our backs, and urged
us to abandon the idea of going alone.   The commander
declared that nothing would give him so much satisfaction
as to accompany us with his squadron, but without the
permission of Parliament he could not venture on the
undertaking.   Numerous and startling events had taken
place since we sailed from Scilly.   News of the latter had
been brought by a large ship which had joined the
squadron from England.   Jersey, though gallantly de-
fended by Sir George Carteret, had been captured by a
fleet under Admiral Blake.   Commodore Young had fallen
in with the Dutch fleet, the admiral of which refusing to
lower his flag, the commodore had attacked it, and after a
sharp action had compelled the Dutchmen to strike.

"Those were brave deeds, but the fighting was mere
child's play compared to what took place afterwards,"
exclaimed Captain Harman, commanding the *Diamond*, the
frigate which had just come out from England. " It was
thought after the lesson they had received that the Dutch
would not again flaunt their flag in British waters, but
before long the Dutch Admiral, Van Tromp, made his
appearance in the Downs with a fleet of forty-two men-of-
war and frigates. At the time Admiral Blake was cruising
in the *James* off Rye, when the news reached him that Van
Tromp was off Dover.   He at once made sail.   Upon
reaching the Straits he saw the Dutch fleet standing out to
sea.   Suddenly, however, they tacked and stood towards
him.   He had but fifteen ships, but he had sent to Admiral
Bourne to join him with a squadron of eight ships.   They
were, however, not yet in sight; still, our ships were
larger, with more men than were on board the Dutch, so

that the disproportion of strength was not so great as might appear. Tromp, who led the van in the *Brederode*, fired into the *James*, when Admiral Blake instantly ordered his gunners to return the salute. The fight then became general. The *James* bore the brunt of the action. Her masts were knocked away, her hull riddled, and many officers and men were killed.

"Young Robert Blake, who—Vice-Admiral Penn being absent—took command of the *Triumph*, greatly distinguished himself, succouring his uncle and contributing much to the success of the day.

"From four o'clock to nightfall the battle raged, when Admiral Bourne arriving with his squadron turned the scale, and the Dutchmen took to flight, leaving two ships in our hands, while the rest were more or less disabled, with two hundred and fifty prisoners and many more killed.

"Admiral Blake thus remained master of the narrow seas, and in less than a month had captured forty rich prizes from the Dutch, which he sent into the Thames. As the Government were well assured that the Dutch would try to revenge themselves, great preparations were made for renewing the contest, and in one month one hundred and five vessels carrying three thousand nine hundred and sixty-one guns were placed under Admiral Blake's command.

"As sufficient seamen were not to be found, two regiments of foot were sent on board the fleet.

"The admiral then sailed north to capture a large fleet of Dutch herring busses, in order to obtain fish for his crews. No less than six hundred fell into his hands, but, unwilling to injure the families of the poor men depending upon them, he contented himself with taking only a small portion from each buss, and forbidding them again to fish in British waters. They were convoyed by twelve Dutch men-of-war, which he attacked, sinking three and capturing the other nine.

" A portion of the busses he pursued to the Danish coast. While still in those northern seas, several of his ships having been sent to the Orkneys to repair, he received news that Tromp was on his way to attack him, with a fleet greatly outnumbering his.

" The evening of the 5th of August was drawing on, when as the admiral was cruising near Fair Isle, about midway between the Orkneys and Shetlands, he caught sight of the Dutch Fleet. Instant preparations for battle were made, but before a gun was fired, the admiral observing that a heavy gale was coming on, threw out a signal to his ships to prepare for it.

" Down came the tempest with fearful force. The seamen instead of having to fight with mortal foes had now to contend with the raging tempest. The wind shifted to the north north-west, gaining every instant additional force. The sea ran mountains high, filling the air with sheets of foam, through which one ship could scarcely distinguish the other as they were tossed and tumbled by the raging waves. The coming darkness increased the horrors of the scene. Admiral Blake collecting his ships in time, steered for the southward of Shetland, under the shelter of which he remained secure during the height of the tempest. No sooner had it abated than he pursued the sorely battered Dutchmen, capturing many before they escaped into port. The Dutch, after this, knowing that Admiral Blake was waiting for them, did not for some time put again to sea. While he was cruising in the Channel, expecting their appearance, news was brought him that the Spaniards were besieging Dunkirk, but that the French king had sent a fleet for its relief. Believing it was to the interests of England that it should fall, lest the Dutch admiral should make it the basis of operations against the towns on the opposite coast of England, he resolved to go and attack the French fleet.

"The admiral led the way in the *Resolution*, followed by the *Sovereign*, the largest of our ships, carrying eleven hundred men and eighty-eight guns. He first attacked the *Donadieu*, commanded by a Knight of Malta, and boarding her, pike in hand, took her in a few minutes, while the *Sovereign* with her terrible broadside sank one of the royal frigates and dismantled five others.

"So desperate was the onslaught, that in a few hours every French ship had been sunk or captured, the prizes being carried into the Downs. Scarcely was this victory gained when the Dutch fleet, under Admirals De Witt and De Ruiter, were sighted off the North Foreland. Admiral Blake, without waiting for the rest of his fleet, which were astern, immediately ordered each ship to engage as she came up, and leading the way attacked De Witt's line. Tremendous were the broadsides exchanged. As night came on the Dutch retreated, having suffered severely, the masts of many of the ships being shot away and vast numbers of men being slain. The next morning the Dutch seemed disposed to renew the bloody work of the previous day, but their courage failed as the English admiral bore down, and putting up their helms, they ran for their native coast, followed by Blake until the shallowness of the water compelled him to desist from pursuit. The Dutch, though thus signally defeated, would, it was thought, again attempt to regain their lost power on the return of spring, and information was received that their most celebrated admiral, Van Tromp, would take command of their fleet. It was not supposed, however, that it would be ready until the spring.

"No sooner had our ships been dispersed to their winter

stations, than Tromp appeared with a fleet of more than a hundred sail off the Goodwin Sands.

"Admiral Blake, who was still on board the *Triumph*, on hearing of this, collected all the ships he could get, and stood out of Dover to attack the Dutch. For the whole of that winter's day the two admirals watched each other, each endeavouring to obtain the weather gauge.

"A dark and tempestuous night then coming on separated the fleets of both ships. The following day the weather moderated. Still for some hours the *Triumph* and Tromp's flag-ship the *Brederode* kept manoeuvring, until late in the afternoon the Dutchman made a sudden attempt to take the English admiral at a disadvantage. Blake, however, by suddenly luffing-up crossed the bow of the *Brederode*, followed by the *Garland*, against which ship the *Brederode* ran with a tremendous crash, when both became hotly engaged. The *Bonaventura*, a trader of only thirty guns, gallantly came up to the rescue of the *Garland*. While thus fighting, Admiral Evertz attacked the latter ship, the whole four being alongside each other, when after a desperate struggle, more than half the crews of the two English ships being killed and wounded, they were boarded and carried by the Dutchmen. Meanwhile the *Triumph*, *Vanguard*, and *Victory* were fighting desperately with twenty of the enemy's ships, frequently almost surrounded before many of the rest of the fleet had gone into action. The men stood bravely to their guns, although numbers were falling on their decks, and fought their way on, until the night coming down put an end to the battle.

"The following morning a thick fog prevented the enemy being seen, and with his shattered fleet Admiral Blake thought it wise to retire up the Thames to repair damages and collect his ships in readiness again to encounter the enemy. Such was the last action which was fought before we left England," continued the officer; " but I am ashamed to say that Tromp was seen vauntingly sailing up and down the Channel with a broom at his masthead, as if he had swept the English from the sea."

CHAPTER X.

A BITTER DISAPPOINTMENT.

THE news brought by the *Diamond* made the officers and crews of the squadron eager to return to England to avenge the insult put upon the English flag by Van Tromp. The crew of the *Good Hope*, Royalists as many of them had been, shared equally in the feeling. So would Lancelot and I, had we not had a more sacred duty to perform; but when we mentioned our plan to the commodore, he positively forbade our making the attempt.

"It would be the height of madness to venture in your small ship on the Barbary coast," he repeated. "Before you could explain your object, she would be captured, and you and your crew would be carried into slavery."

For a long time we entreated him in vain to allow us to prosecute our undertaking. At last he said—

"I will allow you to go, provided your people are ready to accompany you after you have clearly explained to them the dangers of the enterprise; but I again warn you of your certain fate. My advice is that you should return to England, make known the sad condition of your own friends, and numberless other Christian captives in Barbary, and I have little doubt that as soon as we have thrashed the Dutch, Admiral Blake will be sent out to compel the corsairs to give up their prisoners."

The only course open to us was to follow the commodore's advice. Bitter was our disappointment when our crew declined further to prosecute the undertaking.

In vain Martin and Dick urged them to fulfil their engagement, supported by Mr. Aylett.

They were ready to fight with a prospect of success, but they had no desire to be made slaves, or to lose their lives in a hopeless cause, they answered.

I cannot describe our feelings; we did not possess even the means of communicating with the captives, and letting them know that we were making efforts for their liberation. At last the signal was made to weigh anchor, and the *Good Hope*, with several ships ordered home, set sail for England.

Having met a Dutch fleet which we beat off, though they left us sorely battered, and encountered a fearful storm which well nigh sent the *Good Hope* to the bottom, we at length reached Plymouth in a sinking state. There the shipwrights pronounced the *Good Hope* unfit again to go to sea.

This was the climax of our disappointments, for we had not the means of obtaining another vessel.

"Cheer up, shipmates!" exclaimed Dick Harvey "I'll try and induce my father to help us. He will rejoice to see me back safe, and you too, for he has a sincere regard for you, and is grateful for the service you rendered him."

Finding that Mr. Harvey had gone to London, we repaired thither, taking Martin and Mr. Aylett with us.

Mr. Harvey was glad to see his son, and treated Lancelot and me with great kindness; his means, however, would not allow him, he said, to purchase a ship, but he advised us to repair to Queensborough, in the island of Sheppey, where Admiral Blake was busily employed in fitting out a fleet to attack the Dutch.

That we might not miss the opportunity of joining the fleet. we immediately went on board a hoy which was going down the river. We found the roads crowded with men-of-war. sixty sail at least, beside frigates, all busily engaged in taking stores, and powder and shot on board. The admiral's flag was flying at the mast-head of the *Triumph*. As we reached her deck, we found him surrounded by officers, to whom he was issuing orders. It was some time before we could approach to pay our respects. He recognised us at once, and holding out his hand, shook ours warmly, listening with much interest to the account we gave him of our adventures.

"You have come in the nick of time," he said. "We sail to-morrow in search of the Dutch. You shall all serve on board. There's work to be done, and I have not too many officers or men to do it. After we have thrashed the Dutch. I promise you, should my life be spared, to inflict due chastisement on the Barbary corsairs, and to endeavour to recover your friends."

More than this we could not expect, and we at once zealously set about performing the duties assigned to us. Lancelot and Aylett were appointed to act as lieutenants, and the admiral directed Dick and me to remain by him ready to signal his orders to the rest of the fleet, to carry messages, or to perform any other duties he might require.

On inquiring for his nephew, young Robert Blake, we found that he had been appointed to command the *Hampshire*, a thirty-four gun ship; but as no boat could be spared. we were unable to pay him a visit.

Near us lay the *Speaker*, Vice-Admiral Penn, and the *Fairfax*, Rear-Admiral Lawson, while the other ships were commanded by the best captains in the navy.

At daybreak next morning we sailed. Soon after we got round the South Foreland, a fleet was descried from the mast-head of the *Triumph*, standing out from the land. The hearts of all on board beat high, for we believed that the enemy were in sight. But the strangers tacking soon showed English colours, and we found that it was the Plymouth squadron, which had been sent out to join us.

Thus, with eighty ships, we stood down Channel, with a north-westerly wind, until we had passed the Isle of Wight. When nearly up to the Bill of Portland, the *Triumph* leading, just as day broke the look-out aloft shouted—

" A fleet ahead, a fleet ahead ! away to the south-west."

There was no doubt now that the Dutch were in sight. The officer of the watch ordered me to call the admiral.

With a cheerful countenance he rose, and quickly dressing himself, came on deck, going to the fore-top, where I accompanied him, that he might take a perfect survey of the enemy with whom he was about to engage.

On one side of us was the *Speaker*, on the other the *Fairfax*, both within hail, and about a score of other ships forming our vanguard ; but Admiral Monk, with the main body of the fleet, was still some four or five miles astern. Though we could see them, they were not visible to the Dutch admiral, Van Tromp, who, having under him many other celebrated captains, was known to command the Dutch fleet.

The sun, which was just rising above the horizon, clearing away the wintry mist, showed us the whole shining ocean covered with sails, a large proportion nearest to us being men-of-war, but fully three hundred others could be counted beyond them, which were supposed to be merchant vessels.

Undaunted by the overwhelming numbers opposed to him, without waiting for the rest of the fleet to come up, Admiral Blake pressed on with all sail to attack the enemy.

The leading ship of the Hollanders was recognised as the *Brederode*, carrying the flag of Van Tromp. Close astern of us came the *Speaker* and the *Fairfax*, the rest of the vanguard not being far behind.

"He hasn't got the broom aloft," whispered Dick to me, as he stood close to the admiral on the after castle watching the enemy. "If he had we should soon knock it away."

"We shall, I hope, before long knock away his masts," I answered. "But see, he is getting closer; before another minute is over the fight will begin."

We were now so steering, that we should speedily pass along the Dutch line, which only waited for the *Triumph* to get within range to open fire.

Presently a puff of smoke issued from the bows of the *Brederode*, and almost before the shot aimed at us could strike, the *Triumph* opened fire from the whole of her broadside. The *Speaker* and the *Fairfax* followed our example, as did the other ships, receiving in return the broadside of the entire Dutch fleet.

The Dutch admiral, with the wind free, shot by us, delivering his fire from one broadside, then tacking under our lee, discharged the other with tremendous effect, wounding our masts and spars, riddling our canvas and rigging, and strewing our decks with killed and wounded.

Other Dutch ships imitated the example of their admiral and steered down upon us, when we should have fared ill from odds so overwhelming, had not Admiral Penn, followed by two other vessels, come to the rescue and drawn off the attention of the enemy to themselves.

As we got out from the circle of fire we could better see what was going on, though all the time we were hotly engaged with one or more of the enemy.

Dick and I immediately reported every circumstance to the admiral. Now the *Assistance* was boarded by the

Dutch. Now two ships ran alongside the *Prosperous*, and in spite of the valour of her crew, she was captured by the enemy. The *Oak* shared the same fate, though her people fought long and bravely.

On my reporting what I had seen to the admiral,

"We must go to their help," he exclaimed, and ordering the master to steer for them, we furiously attacked the ships to which they had struck.

We had, however, to contend with the rest of the Dutch fleet, and it appeared to be going hard with us. In spite, however, of almost overwhelming odds against us, we and the other ships of the vanguard fought on. Often I turned my eyes to the eastward, but could discover no signs of the advance of the fleet, the thick wreaths of smoke often preventing me from seeing to any distance. At length, however, I saw the rays of the sun falling on their white canvas, and ship after ship appeared. It was the white division, led by General Monk; as they arrived they gallantly opened their broadsides on the Dutchmen, increasing the fearful uproar. On every side the sea appeared covered with shattered spars and planks. Now a noble ship was wrapt in flames, now I caught sight of the tall masts of another sinking beneath the surface as she and her crew went down to the depths below.

The ship we had rescued was the *Prosperous*, of forty guns, commanded by Captain Baker; but he and many of his crew lay dead on the deck. Admiral De Ruiter, who had attacked her, was himself almost surrounded, and would have been captured had not several of the enemy under Admiral Evertz come to his rescue. The *Speaker*, not far off, was meantime fiercely assaulted, and reduced almost to a wreck. First her foremast fell, then her mizen-mast was shot away, and she would have been captured had not several ships been sent to her assistance.

A Dutch ship within sight, the *Ostrich*, commanded by Captain Krink, with her rigging cut to pieces and her sails in tatters, fought on until her masts were shot away by the board, when two of our ships ran alongside and carried her. It appearing impossible that she could swim, her captain with the survivors of his officers and crew were hastily dragged on board their captors, and the *Ostrich* was deserted.

On the other side of us another Dutch ship, commanded by Captain De Port, was attacked by two of ours, and from the way they handled their guns, in a short time it was very evident that they had reduced her to a sinking state.

Another brave Hollander, Captain Swers, seeing her condition, hastened to her relief; but he came too late, and our ship turning on him, ere long reduced him to the same condition as his countryman.

As I stood on our lofty after castle I could look down on the fight, and saw the brave De Port, though lying on the deck desperately wounded, flourishing his hanger and shouting to his crew to resist. Before the English could get on board, down went his ship, carrying him and his men with her. Scarcely had she disappeared than Swers' ship was seen to be sinking, but more fortunate than his brother captain, he and several of his officers were rescued by their victors.

In other directions we could see that several of the Dutch ships had struck their flags. Four of ours had been boarded by the enemy, but afterwards recaptured. Among them was the. *Sampson*, commanded by Captain Bullon. So fearfully had she suffered, he and the greater portion of his crew having been slain, that the admiral ordered the remainder to be taken out, and allowed her to drift away.

We ourselves, having endured the brunt of the battle well nigh from sunrise to sunset, had also suffered fearfully.

AN ENGAGEMENT WITH THE DUTCH.

I was standing near the admiral, when a shot struck down Mr. Sparrow, his secretary, by his side, and our commander, Captain Ball, also fell shortly afterwards. As I looked along the decks I could see them covered with dead and wounded, there being scarcely men left sufficient to carry the latter below, the survivors having to work on at the guns.

Still the battle raged, and round shot continued tearing along our decks. One came whizzing close to me. Turning at the same moment, I saw that the admiral was struck. I sprang forward to save him ere he fell to the deck.

"It's a mere flesh wound," he replied to my inquiries. "Let not the men suppose that I am hurt," and taking a handkerchief, he, with my assistance, bound it round the wound and resumed his upright position, cheering on the men as was his wont.

The same shot had torn away part of the buff coat of General Deane, who had remained on board to aid his old comrade in arms.

I often, as may be supposed, looked out to see how it was faring with my old friends. Though many were laid low by their sides, still they remained unhurt.

The evening of that short winter's day was approaching, when our admiral, perceiving the shattered condition of a large number of the enemy's ships, and that no less than eight had been sunk, blown up, or captured, directed the fastest frigates nearest to us to make all sail and cut off the fleet of traders, which had been hove to in the distance during the day.

This done he kept his eagle eye on Tromp, who shortly afterwards was seen to throw out signals to steer to the south-east, followed by a considerable portion of his fleet, evidently with the intention of protecting the traders.

Seeing their admiral apparently retreating, the rest of the

fleet took to hasty flight, on which from every English ship arose a loud shout of triumph, the crews for the moment forgetting the heavy price at which the day's victory had been gained.

As we passed in view of the captured ships, the scene which their decks presented was sufficient to sicken our hearts. None of the brave Dutchmen had yielded until the last hope was gone. Fore and aft lay the mangled corpses of the slain, while the shattered bulwarks and even the stumps of the masts were bespattered with blood and gore.

Though a battle was no new event to me, I turned away appalled and sickened at the sight. Not only were our crews exhausted, but few of our ships were in a condition to pursue the enemy, and great was our fear that they would escape during the night; but as the sun disappeared beneath the western horizon the wind dropped, and both squadrons lay becalmed on the smooth ocean. All the boats which could float were immediately lowered, and the wounded being placed in them, they were rowed to shore, where hospitals had been prepared for their reception. General Deane and others entreated the admiral to land and obtain that attention to his wound which he was so anxious to afford to others.

"No, no, my friends," he answered, pointing to the lights from the Dutch ships, which streamed across the wintry sea. "With the enemy out there, it is no time for me to seek for rest," and before retiring to his cabin he issued orders that every effort should be made to prepare the fleet for another battle on the morrow.

Not a man or boy able to work turned in that night, for all were employed in stopping shot holes, knotting and splicing rigging, bending new sails, and repairing the tackles of the guns.

The survivors of the crew of the *Sampson* came on board the *Triumph* to assist, but even the united crews scarcely made up the ship's complement.

As daylight broke, a light breeze enabled us to make sail, and followed by the whole fleet, the *Triumph* stood for the enemy, who were steering under all sail to the eastward. Soon afterwards we saw ahead a ship floating which we made out to be Dutch, and as we came up to her, we perceived that she was the *Ostrich*, the ship of the brave Krink, and terrible was the spectacle she exhibited. The masts, shot away by the board, hung trailing over the side, not a human being stood alive on her blood-stained decks, which were covered with corpses, lying were they had fallen when she had been abandoned on the previous day.

There was no time to take her in tow, and we left her afloat on the ocean, the coffin of her hapless crew; then onward we pressed under every sail we could carry. It was not until noon that we were near enough to open fire, and it was two o'clock, Dungeness being in sight, before the whole fleet got into action.

To give an account of the battle would be to describe the scenes of the previous day. The gallant De Ruiter was well-nigh captured, and would have been so had not another brave Dutch captain come to his rescue.

Well and courageously did our captains do their duty, imitating the example of the admiral, and carrying their ships as best they could alongside the Hollanders. Five or six of their men-of-war were that evening taken, besides which many others were fearfully mauled.

Another night came down upon the world of waters, bitterly cold, yet calm and clear, enabling us to distinguish the lights of the Dutch ships, now retreating towards Boulogne.

The second night was spent like the first, and a third

day found us still in sight of our unconquered foe. The wind had shifted to the southward, preventing their escape, and our frigates being again despatched with all canvas set, bore down on the richly-laden merchantmen, while we once more assailed the men-of-war.

In vain Van Tromp fought with courage and desperation, endeavouring while retreating to protect the merchantmen. Already in the distance we could see the frigates playing havoc among the traders, which were thrown into the wildest confusion, numbers running against each other, some hauling down their flags, others contriving to escape.

As we pressed on, we could see the other English war ships at length got among them, and several ran up to us with the intention, it was seen, of yielding, and thereby delaying us in our pursuit of Van Tromp.

"We are not to be delayed by such a device," exclaimed the admiral. "Make the signal, Bracewell, to all the ships of war to press on regardless of the traders. The frigates will look after them.; they can with ease be picked up when we have finally defeated Van Tromp and his captains."

Thus we continued the pursuit until again night was approaching, when Van Tromp with the remnant of his fleet was seen to run in under the French coast, where he dropped anchor and furled his sails. Before we could reach him night came down upon us.

It was a night very different to the last. The wind was blowing strong from the southward, threatening every instant to increase into a hard gale. Clouds obscured the sky, and darkness and mist shrouded the enemy from view.

Our fleet dropped anchor to the southward of Cape Grisnez, when every man who could keep his eyes open was employed in repairing damages.

The pilots asserted that with the wind as it was then

blowing from the north-east, and with the tide as it would be running during the morning, the Dutch would find it impossible to weather Cape Blanchnez, and we looked forward eagerly to the next day, in the anticipation of inflicting a final and crushing blow on our enemy.

Alas! and such is war, though I thought but little at the time of its sinfulness, its horrors, and the sufferings it entails, not only on the combatants but on those at home, their wives and families. That lesson I was to learn in subsequent years from the son of one of our admirals, who pointed out to me its iniquity, and how contrary it is to all the teaching of the Gospel. Even on lower principles I had already seen the folly of that war between two Protestant nations, who ought to have continued to advance each other's commercial prosperity, and more than all, to resist the machinations of the sworn enemies of the faith.

CHAPTER XI.

HEN morning broke, gloomy and tempestuous, and we stood out from under the lee of Cape Grisnez, so as to get a view of the coast, where we had seen the Dutch anchor, great was our disappointment on discovering that not a mast was visible. It was very evident that, favoured by darkness, they had slipped out with the last of the flood, and were by this time amid the sandbanks and shallows off the Flushing coast. The gale increasing, we now threw out the order for the fleet to bear away and steer for the Isle of Wight, under the shelter of which we at length brought up. On counting our prizes, we found that we had captured no less than nineteen men-of-war, and not under fifty merchantmen, which had been carried to different ports. Three Dutch captains had been taken prisoners and seven slain. Even though still suffering from his wound, the admiral went on shore, not to take a part in the rejoicings with which our victory was welcomed throughout the land, but to visit the hospitals and see that the wounded men were properly cared for. I accompanied him from ward to

ward. He had a kind word for every one, and many an
eye was filled with tears as he thanked them for the noble
way in which they had fought for their country, and the
glorious victory they had won.

Refusing to go home, though he required rest more than
any one, he continued to superintend the repairs of the
fleet.

I cannot dwell on the events which followed. We again
sailed in April with a hundred ships for the Texel, where
we drove the Dutch fleet back into port, capturing fifty
dogers. The admiral hearing that Van Tromp had gone
northward, to convoy a fleet of merchantmen, we sailed in
pursuit with part of the fleet, leaving Admiral Lawson in
command of the larger portion. Missing the Dutch, we
once again steered southward, when just as June had commenced, a fast frigate brought intelligence that Van Tromp
had appeared in the Downs, and that another fierce battle
was hourly expected between him and the English fleet
under Admirals Penn and Lawson.

Setting all sail, we pressed on before a northerly breeze,
when the sound of firing reached our ears.

Robert Blake in the *Hampshire* was ahead. How we
envied him! At length, some way to the southward of
Yarmouth, the two fleets of England and Holland appeared
in sight, hotly engaged. With every stitch of canvas set
below and aloft, he sailed on into action, firing his broadsides with terrific effect into the enemy's ships.

We followed, eager to engage, as did the rest of the
squadron, and were soon in the midst of it. Among the
ships we perceived the *James*, Vice-Admiral Penn, alongside
the well known *Brederode*, with Van Tromp's flag flying
aloft. The Dutch had endeavoured to board the *James*,
but were now being driven back, with fearful slaughter,
and already scores of British seamen, slashing and cutting

with their hangers, had gained her deck when a terrific explosion was heard. Up rose the deck of the Dutch ship, sending into the air the mangled forms of the boarders with the shivered fragments of planks.

The *James* cast off from her foe, it being believed that Van Tromp with his crew were about to founder, but the smoke clearing away, we saw them rushing up from below, with the admiral at their head. Before he could be captured, lowering a boat, he pulled away for a frigate which lay near, and was seen sailing through his fleet, assuring his followers of his wonderful escape.

But his efforts and those of his vice-admiral were in vain. Hard pressed by our ships, they ere long took to flight, and steered for Ostend, leaving eleven of their men-of-war in our hands, besides six sunk, two blown up, and one burnt, and nearly fourteen hundred prisoners, including a vice-admiral, two rear-admirals, and six captains.

The battle was won, but so shattered were our ships that, unable to pursue the enemy, we were compelled to put into harbour. Not until he saw his fleet at anchor would Admiral Blake allow himself to be carried on shore, when he invited me to accompany him to his country house of Knoll, near Bridgwater.

Dick, I should have said, had been summoned home by his father, but I bade farewell for a time to Lancelot, as also to old Martin, who, in spite of his years, preferred remaining on board to taking his ease on shore.

"Who knows but that the ship may be sent out to the Mediterranean, and if so, that I may have the chance of hearing of Mistress Audrey and Margaret, and Mr. Kerridge and his daughter?" he said.

"For that reason I ought to remain," I answered; "but the admiral has promised, should any ship sail for those parts, to let me go in her, and as he knows everything that takes place, I am not afraid of missing the chance.

"And very right, Master Ben, that you should take a holiday. You look as thin as a line, and I have been afraid that you'd wear yourself out before your time."

So I set off with my noble patron. Great was the contrast which his life in that quiet abode presented to the uproar of battle and tempest, in which so many of his days had of late been passed. His board was frugal. His mornings were passed among his books or in writing letters, in which I assisted him; a long walk when his strength was sufficiently restored through the green fields and woods; his evenings in the society of a few chosen friends, when his conversation was chiefly on religious matters or on the affairs of state. To me the change was beneficial in the extreme. I felt refreshed in mind and body, still my thoughts were often far away with my sister and friends, captives still, as I believed, in Barbary.

The tranquil existence the admiral was enjoying was greatly disturbed by the news of another complete victory gained over the Dutch by Admirals Monk, Penn, and Lawson. The battle had lasted, like the former, for well-nigh three days. It was the last Van Tromp was destined to fight.

On the third day, while still leading on his fleet, a musket ball entered his heart, and his captain hearing of his death took to flight, pursued by the victors, who, it is sad to say, had received orders from Monk to give no quarter, but to destroy every ship and their hapless crews as they were overtaken. The captains and their crews, however, disregarding the sanguinary order, picked up several hundred Dutchmen from their sinking ships.

I was thankful to get a letter from Lancelot describing the fight, assuring me of his and Martin's safety. Ere long we heard of the arrival of ambassadors from the States General, sueing for peace, when among other matters they agreed to lower their flag to that of England whenever it should be seen flying. I must pass over several months, when once more Admiral Blake went afloat in command of a fleet of twenty-four sail, and hoisted his flag on board the *St. George*, a new ship of sixty guns and three hundred and fifty men. Lancelot and Martin had joined her, and Dick soon after came on board, having obtained leave from his father once more to go afloat. We three were thus again united. Great was our satisfaction to learn that the Mediterranean was the ultimate destination of the fleet, though its other objects, for political reasons, were not made known.

At the same time that we sailed, another still larger fleet went down Channel under command of Admiral Penn, having General Venables and a body of troops on board. Its destination was the West Indies, where it was to attack the colonies of Spain, while we were to capture and destroy her fleets on her coasts. This work, however, was not to commence for the present. We having reached the roadstead of Cadiz, found there a Dutch fleet. No sooner was the red cross seen flying from our mastheads, than the Dutch admiral lowered his flag.

"The Hollanders have learned a lesson they are not in a hurry to forget," observed the admiral, as he walked the deck, while we came to an anchor.

A French squadron paid our flag the same respect, while on shore the admiral was treated with every possible consideration by the Spanish authorities, as well as by the officials of all nations.

While here we received information that many more vessels had been captured by the Barbary States. The Pope and Grand Duke of Tuscany also had given offence to the Commonwealth, by allowing Prince Rupert to sell his prizes in their ports.

Those combative monks, the Knights of Malta, also sworn foes to those they chose to call heretics, had captured several English merchantmen, while the Duke of Guise was threatening Naples, which State, then in alliance with England, it was deemed important to protect.

We had work enough thus cut out for us, and as soon as provisions had been obtained we sailed, and passing through the Straits of Gibraltar without molestation, we directed our course for Naples.

We there found that the Duke of Guise had taken his departure, but in what direction we could not discover. We therefore steered northward along the coast of Italy until we came off Leghorn. Dropping anchor, the admiral sent an envoy to the Duke of Tuscany, demanding redress to the owners of such vessels as had been sold by the corsair princes.

The Duke hesitated, declaring that he must refer the matter to the Pope of Rome, at which the admiral, smiling scornfully, observed that "it was not the Pope's business, and that he would presently have to look out for himself."

We had just before received intelligence of the alarm our appearance had caused in Rome. Monks had been walking in procession, many persons had been burying their treasures, and the wealthy had fled from the city, believing that ere long it would be pillaged by the English.

The Grand Duke, not wishing to have Leghorn battered down, yielded to the demands of our admiral, who then despatched the envoy to the Pope. In vain that priestly potentate endeavoured to excuse himself, but his subjects had undoubtedly bought the illegal prizes, and at last, to avoid the threatened consequences of refusal, he sent the money demanded on board, twenty thousand pistoles,

M

"which," as the admiral observed, "was probably the first cash which had ever been transferred from the Papal coffers to the treasury of England."

This was not the only satisfactory task performed by our admiral. He wrote to the Grand Duke, urging him in forcible terms to permit the English and other Protestants settled in his domains liberty to keep the Bible in their houses, and to follow their own form of worship, a privilege which had hitherto been denied them.

While we lay off Leghorn two Algerine cruisers came in with a flag of truce, bringing a number of English captives liberated by the Dey in order to appease the wrath of the English.

"It is well," said our admiral, as he received the liberated persons; "but let the Dey understand while an Englishman remains in bonds I shall not be content."

Lancelot and I eagerly questioned the freed captives, in the hopes of possibly gaining information about our friends; but they replied that the distance between the two States was so great that they were aware only of the fact that many English were held captive in Tunis. The admiral had from the first promised that he would pay that pirate city a visit, and use every means to discover and liberate our friends. We now hoped that he would without delay carry out his intention. But another disappointment occurred. Just as we were about to sail, the plague brought from the Levant broke out on board, and the admiral himself was stricken down by the fell disease. Others suffered, and for many weeks, until the admiral recovered, we were unable to sail.

Although with the cold of winter the disease disappeared, a storm kept us still longer at anchor; but at length the wind proving favourable we sailed for Tunis, and ere long came in sight of its two powerful castles of Goletta and

Porto Ferino. Bringing up beyond reach of their guns, the admiral despatched a messenger to the Dey, demanding the release of all prisoners and the restoration of the numerous prizes lately captured, or their value if destroyed.

The Dey in return sent an envoy on board the *St. George*, who, though he professed to wish for peace, declared that his master would not give up the prizes.

While negotiations were going on, we sailed close up to the castle of Porto Ferino, piloted by Lieutenant Aylett, that the admiral might obtain an idea of its strength. He then (the envoy being sent on shore) sailed away with the larger ships, leaving Captain Stayner with the smaller frigates to watch the entrance of the harbour.

Lancelot and I could not help expressing our disappointment to each other; we soon found, however, that the admiral had no intention of abandoning the undertaking, but that it was necessary to obtain provisions before we commenced operations, our stock having run short.

We now steered for Cagliari in Sardinia, where we lay while vessels were despatched in all directions to obtain bread, and the ships in harbour were being refitted. Our hearts beat high when once more the tall minarets and domes of the pirate city appeared in sight, for we made no doubt that the Dey would yield, and that we should ere long recover our friends. Again the admiral sent an officer on shore, repeating his former demands and requesting water for his ships.

The Dey insolently replied that " there stood his castles of Porto Ferino and Goletta, and until the English could carry them off in their ships, nothing should they have from him."

" Let the Dey understand that such conduct shall not go unpunished," answered the admiral to the barbarian envoy, his anger rising, and his usually calm eye flashing fire.

"God has given water to all His creatures, and the sin which one commits who refuses it to another is great indeed."

No sooner had the envoy taken his departure than, to the surprise of all, the admiral ordered the fleet to sail away from the harbour, not leaving a ship behind.

"Can the admiral really intend thus to allow the pirates to escape with impunity ? " said Dick to Lancelot and me. as we watched the Moorish city recede from our eyes. "I much fear that your relatives will be left to languish in hopeless captivity."

"Have you sailed so many years with our good commander, and yet can fancy such a thing?" exclaimed Martin, who overheard the remark. "Depend upon it, he has his reasons, and I shrewdly guess wishes to throw the pirates off their guard. Rest assured before long we shall get a nearer sight of Tunis than we have hitherto had."

Notwithstanding what Martin said, we steered on until we once more entered the Bay of Cagliari. We had good reason, however, to believe that the admiral intended after all to attack Tunis. Orders were issued to all the ships to prepare for some severe work.

At length, after well-nigh a week had passed, we made the signal to weigh anchor, and the whole fleet before a light northerly breeze stood under full sail towards the Bay of Tunis.

Just as the evening of the 3rd of April, 1655, was approaching, we stood into the bay, where we brought up, the now well-known towers and minarets of Tunis in sight. The night which came on might be the last we knew for many a brave fellow. It was spent in preparation for the work we were destined to undertake the next day. Ere the sun rose a gun from the flag-ship was fired as a signal to the crews of the whole fleet to offer up prayer to Almighty

God for protection and success in the struggle about to commence in our righteous cause.

It was a solemn time. Not a sound was heard except the voices of the ministers until those of the congregations joined in prayer, or burst forth into a hymn of praise to the all-powerful One whose protection they sought. Then rising from our knees we weighed anchor, the sails were let fall, the guns run out, and, led by the *Newcastle*, which was quickly followed by other frigates, the big ships stood into the harbour. Of these the *St. Andrew* was the first. Close astern came the *Plymouth*, and we in the *St. George* followed in her wake, not casting anchor until we had got within musket shot of the batteries, nor was a shot fired until we had furled sails.

So astonished were the barbarians that their artillery remained mute. It was not for long; we setting the example, every ship opened with her broadside, to which the pirates speedily replied, their shot coming crashing on board through our bulwarks, or tearing their way between our masts and rigging. And now commenced the most tremendous din and uproar our ears had ever heard, the echoes of the guns reverberating among the crumbling walls and falling houses.

For two hours the battle raged, the sky obscured, and the castles and batteries almost concealed by the dense masses of smoke, on which a lurid glare was reflected by the flames belched forth from the guns. The smoke blown in the faces of the pirates tended to conceal the ships from their sight, and prevented them aiming their pieces with accuracy. Not for an instant did our fire slacken, until the guns in the batteries were dismounted or burst, or the gunners killed or driven from their post.

Within us, higher up the harbour, lay a squadron of nine stout ships. While the bombardment was taking place the admiral called Captain Stokes to his side.

" Now is the time to carry out your plan," he said. " You, Bracewell and Kerridge, may accompany Captain Stokes," he added.

Each ship had before received an order, at a certain time to send her long-boat with a picked crew, bringing torches, hand-grenades, and other combustibles.

They now arrived. We took our places in the long-boat of the *St. George*, and Captain Stokes at once led the way towards the pirate squadron.

For some time we were concealed by the clouds of smoke from the sight of our enemies, and only such shot as passed over the ships came near us, but as we got farther up the harbour we were perceived and assailed by showers of bullets and round shot, fired at us from the corsairs. We pulled on, however, until we were alongside them. The torches were then lighted, and without a moment's delay we began to heave them into the ports of the pirate vessels.

So unexpected was the proceeding, that every ship was set on fire fore and aft, before the crew on deck had perceived what had occurred, and in a few moments the flames were bursting through the hatchways and ports, and encircling the masts and spars. In vain the pirates made the most frantic efforts to extinguish the fire, where-ever they were seen labouring with buckets, the broadsides of the frigates which came up to our assistance drove them away and compelled them to leap overboard. Now every one of the ships was burning furiously, the flames forming huge pyramids of fire.

Leaving them to their fate, which all the efforts of the pirates could not avert, protected by the frigates, we pulled back to the *St. George* to report that the whole of the corsair squadron of nine large ships was utterly destroyed; and as we rowed away, first one and then two or three together blew up with a tremendous explosion, scattering their fragments far and wide, while their keels sank to the bottom of the harbour.

CHAPTER XII.

THE CAPTIVES RESCUED—BLAKE'S EXPLOITS AND DEATH.

ANCELOT and I had formed a plan with Lieutenant Aylett, by which we deemed that it would be possible, though no more than possible, to recover our two sisters, Mr. Kerridge, and Margaret. We had asked permission of the admiral to undertake it. He pointed out the dangers we must encounter.

"Far be it from me ever to refuse my sanction to so righteous an object," he added; "such volunteers as you can obtain may go, and heaven prosper you."

When our design was made known on board the *St George* and *Hampshire*, we might have obtained the whole of the crews of both ships, as well, indeed, as those of the rest of the fleet. On consulting Captain Blake, however, he advised us to take only fifty men; thirty from the flag-ship and the *Hampshire*, and the remainder from among the others of the fleet. We calculated that the whole of the warlike part of the population of Tunis would have been summoned to the defence of the castles and batteries. It was our intention to land while the action continued **about three miles** from the city, at a spot with which Lieutenant Aylett was acquainted, and from thence he knew the road to the residence of the old chief who held our friends captives. We might, he believed, reach the house and be back again to the boats before the Dey could gain intelligence of our expedition, and send any force of strength sufficient to oppose us. Dick, of course, was of the party, and old Martin was as eager as any of the younger men to go; but we tried to persuade him to remain on board, fearing that the fatigue of our march would be more than he could endure. He entreated so hard, however, to be allowed to take part in the recovery of Mistress Audrey that we gave way, and with hanger by his side, pistols in his belt, and a musket over his shoulder, he prepared for the expedition.

While the cannonade was still going forward, we put off in two boats, which kept on the larboard side of one of the frigates, despatched for the service, so that we were unseen from the town. As soon as we had got near the landing-place, the frigate tacked and hove to, while we, pulling rapidly in, leaped on shore, and the boats returned to the frigate, which sailed back as if to rejoin the fleet, but according to orders was ready again to put about to receive us, should our expedition prove successful, on our return.

Led by Lieutenant Aylett, we set out on our march at as fast a rate as our feet could move. Old Martin kept alongside me, showing the activity of many a younger man; fearing, however, that his strength would fail, I begged him to let me carry his musket.

"No, no, Mister Ben," he answered; "I care not, if we get Mistress Audrey and **Margaret back,** whether I fall by the way. I have faced Death in too many shapes to fear him now."

As to the character of the country through which we

passed, I cannot describe it.   I know that there were palm trees, and prickly pears, and other strange shrubs, and rocks covered with creepers, and here and there fields of corn and plantations of fruit trees.   We saw but few people, and those women, children, or old men, who fled at our approach to hide themselves.   Onwards we pushed, regardless of enemies who might be gathering behind— eager only to find the captives and to place them in our midst, when we were prepared to fight our way back against any odds which might oppose us.

My heart bounded as if it would choke me when, on gaining the top of a hill, Lieutenant Aylett exclaimed, pointing ahead—

"There's old Mustapha's house!" but the next instant a sickening feeling came over me, as I dreaded lest those we hoped to find might have been removed.   Without halting for an instant, we rushed down the slope, and so divided our force that we might surround the building.   Orders had been given that not a shot should be fired lest we should wound our friends.   In silence we dashed on, until we were close to the gates, when Lieutenant Aylett cried out—

"Open, open ; we come as friends."

The bars were withdrawn, the gate swung back, when instead of a turbaned Moor, who should we see but old Margaret !   She recognised us at once, as we grasped hands.

"Where are my father and sister?" exclaimed Lancelot.

"Where is my dear Audrey?" I cried.

Before she could reply there arose such a shrieking and shouting from the farther end of the hall that we could scarcely hear her speak.

"Mr. Kerridge is there," she at length said, pointing through an opening into the garden, "and the young ladies

are with Mrs. Mustapha and the other women who are
making all that hubbub there."

"Run, good Margaret, and tell them we are here," I
exclaimed, while Lancelot, like a dutiful son, rushed out
into the garden in search of his father.

Scarcely had he gone than the door at the other end of
the hall opened, and two young boys, as they seemed, sprang
towards us, followed by Margaret. The next instant I had
Audrey in my arms, and was holding the hand of Mistress
Cicely. In spite of their disguise and sunburnt cheeks, I
knew them directly, and in a few words explained how we
had come to rescue them. They were less astonished than
we expected, for the sound of firing had reached their ears,
and they guessed that either the town or pirate ships had
been attacked by a foreign squadron.

Margaret was eagerly talking to Martin, whose attention
was more occupied by Audrey than by what she was saying.
The moment his sense of propriety would allow, coming
forward, he took her hand and poured out the feelings of
his heart at having recovered her.

Before many minutes had passed, the clashing of swords
and Lancelot's voice shouting for assistance reached our
ears. Dick, followed by several of the men, rushed in the
direction he had taken, when they found him defending
himself from the attack of a sturdy old Moor and three
attendants, who, however, on seeing the British seamen
approaching, took to flight. The sailors pursued, and
coming up with the old Moor we were about to cut him
down, when a man with a hoe in his hand sprang out from
behind some bushes, exclaiming—

"Spare his life, friends; though he has kept me in
slavery, and is somewhat a hard taskmaster, we should
return good for evil."

Then, turning to the old Moor, he made a sign to him

that he should remain quiet while he eagerly questioned the seamen. Lancelot by this time had come up. and I saw him spring forward and embrace the stranger, who was, I had no doubt, his long-lost father, although so greatly changed that I had not recognised him.

Such he was, but as not a moment could be spared, after a few words had been exchanged, we were summoned by Lieutenant Aylett to commence our retreat. We did not stop to bid farewell to Mustapha and his family, but placing the two girls with Margaret in our midst, we recommenced our march.

Not a moment did we halt, for we had many miles to travel before we could reach the water, while at any instant we might be attacked by overwhelming numbers of enraged Moors.

My fear was that the rescued ones, unaccustomed to rapid walking, might sink from fatigue, but the joy of having recovered their liberty kept up their strength. The firing had ceased, but as we looked towards the city we could see a cloud of smoke still hanging over it. The last height we had to cross was gained. The sea lay before us, when one of the men on our left flank shouted out he saw a large body of Moors approaching. We all soon saw them, and it seemed doubtful whether we could reach the boats before they were upon us, but as we pushed on the frigate came in view, standing close in with the shore, towards which her guns were directed. The Moors were rushing on, and even at that distance we could hear their savage cries, when the frigate opened fire upon them, compelling them to beat a retreat, while we hastened down the hill and gained the boats which had just come in to receive us. The frigate was obliged to tack, but before the Moors could return we had pulled away beyond the range of their muskets. We were soon on board the frigate, when our arrival caused no small astonishment as well as delight, when it was discovered that we had rescued the captives, and still more so when it was known who they were.

The young ladies, although they had so long worn male attire, were far from feeling at ease on finding themselves among their countrymen, and they entreated to be led below, to avoid the gaze of the seamen.

We should, we feared, have great difficulty in procuring suitable costumes to enable them to appear with satisfaction in public.

"We must apply to the admiral to help us; he can do everything," observed Lancelot. "So don't trouble yourself about the matter, Cicely."

As we stood towards the fleet we saw the line-of-battle ships getting up their anchors, and making sail away from the shore, from which not a gun was now fired. One of the boats conveyed our party to the *St. George,* where the admiral received our friends with the greatest kindness, highly commending us for the way in which we had achieved our undertaking. We found that he intended to inflict no further chastisement on the Dey of Tunis, it being considered that the destruction of his fleet, the ruin of his forts, and the vast number of men who had been slain would induce him to refrain from interfering with English interests in future.

Running along the coast we visited Tripoli, the Dey of which State, taught a lesson by the punishment the ruler of Tunis had received, showed every desire to be on terms of friendship with us. The fleet then proceeded up the Adriatic to pay the Venetians a friendly visit.

Space does not permit me to describe that curious canal-intersected city, where the admiral was received with such honours as are accorded generally only to royal persons. Thanks to his generosity, Cicely and Audrey were here supplied with all the requisite articles of female dress, which were sent on board the day after our arrival, so that they were able to go on shore in their proper characters, and view the wonders of the city.

Leaving the Adriatic we again came off Tunis, when a white flag was seen flying from the castle of Porto Ferino. The Dey immediately acceded to all our demands, and signed a treaty affording advantageous terms to the English.

Thence we stood across to Malta, where the haughty Templars, having heard of the way in which our admiral had exacted reparation, not only from the Grand Duke, but from the Pope himself, at once succumbed and delivered up the ships and their cargoes of which they had despoiled the English merchants. This matter settled, we sailed across to Algiers, the pirate prince of which State immediately sent a present of cattle on board the fleet, and undertook to liberate all English captives in his country at a moderate ransom per head, they being, he observed, the property of private individuals who had purchased them from others, while he undertook never again to molest English traders. To these terms the admiral consented, and in a few days a whole fleet of boats came off, bringing numerous liberated slaves, a large portion of whom had endured the sorrows of captivity for many years, the amount agreed on being paid over to their late masters.

While we lay close in with the shore, we observed one morning a number of persons swimming off towards us. Just as they neared the sides of the ship, several boats, manned by turbaned Moors, were seen pulling away in chase of the fugitives, who now, shouting out in Dutch, entreated us to take them on board.

Our seamen, regardless of the savage war we had lately waged with the Hollanders, hurried to lower down ropes and to drag the swimmers on board. Scarcely were they all on deck than the Algerine boats came alongside, and the Moors demanded the fugitives, affirming that they were their own runaway slaves.

"What!" exclaimed Martin, "give up Christians who have once enjoyed the freedom of an English man-of-war, even though they may be enemies, to pirates and infidels. I don't believe any honest man on board will stand by and see that done. Just bundle the rascally Turks out of the ship, and let them know that when once a man steps under our flag he is free."

The Algerines, with looks of indignation, took their departure, but before long they returned with a message from the Dey, insisting on the terms of the new treaty, by which a certain ransom was to be paid for all liberated captives. On hearing this, Martin suggested that a subscription should be raised to pay the ransom of the Dutchmen. A boat being sent round from ship to ship, the necessary sum was soon collected, the admiral himself paying in proportion to his rank. While we lay off Algiers we heard of the fearful massacre of the Protestants of the Vaudois valley by the soldiers of the Duke of Savoy.

The admiral had received instructions from the Protector to threaten the southern coast of France and Piedmont, should the Duke refuse to make all the reparation in his power. The menace had its due effect, and the Duke gave a pledge not again to interfere with the Christian inhabitants of those lovely valleys. We sailed for the Straits of Gibraltar, calling on the way at Malaga to obtain water and fresh provisions. While a party of our seamen were on shore at that place, a procession carrying the Host, with banners and heathenish figures, passed through the streets, when they not only refused to bow, but mocked and jeered, at which the mob, urged on by a priest, savagely attacked them and drove them back to the boats.

On hearing this, the admiral sent a trumpeter on shore demanding, not that the mob should be punished, but that the priest who had set them on should be delivered up to him.

The governor replied that such a thing as giving up a Catholic priest to heretics had never been heard of, and that he had no power in the case.

On this the admiral replied, "If I fail to see that said priest on the deck of the *St. George* before the lapse of three hours, I will burn your city to the ground."

Within the specified time the priest appeared, when the admiral, summoning witnesses from both sides, heard the case, and decided that the seamen were wrong in mocking, even at the superstitious observances of the natives, but that the priest was also wrong in taking the law into his own hands, instead of sending on board to complain, when the seamen would have been properly punished.

Satisfied that the priest had been placed at his mercy, the admiral, warning him for the future, sent him safely on shore.

On the fleet reaching Cadiz, the admiral finding that he was expected to remain on the coast of Spain to wait for the Silver fleet, offered Mr. Kerridge and his party a passage home in the *Constant Warwick*, by which he was sending off despatches. He at the same time sent Lancelot and me.

"I intend to let you return with your friends, as you require rest after the hard work you have gone through," he said in a kind tone. "You must also take charge of Martin Shobbrok, whose great age and failing strength unfits him for active service. Your names will remain on the books of the *St. George*, and should any captures be made, you will obtain your due share of prize money."

We were both well-nigh overpowered by the admiral's

kindness. Though I desired to remain with him, I felt unwilling to be again separated from Audrey as also from Cicely, as between us a warm attachment had sprung up, though I always before looked on her in the light of a sister.

"But you, sir," I observed, "require rest more than any other person in the fleet."

The admiral smiled faintly as he replied, "While I have life and my country requires my services, I must remain afloat."

Of the homeward voyage I will not speak.

Once more the well-known Start appeared in sight, and the *Constant Warwick* steering for Lyme, we went on shore, thankful to heaven for our safe return to our native land.

Mr. Kerridge forthwith set about placing his affairs, which had suffered from his long absence, in order. Lancelot and I assisting him.

Cicely promised to be mine when the war was over, as I acknowledged; should the admiral summon me, I could not refuse to go.

My sister Audrey had made the same promise to Lancelot; and the ladies could not help laughing and archly remarking to one another that "although they had so long worn a certain pair of garments—considered the exclusive property of men—they were never again likely to put them on."

In the course of the summer Admiral Blake returned to England, but there was no repose for him. In spite of his illness, and the suffering he endured from his wound, he was occupied day after day in visiting the dockyards and arsenals, forwarding the building and repairing of ships, and other duties of his station.

The Commonwealth was at war with Spain. Portugal had not fulfilled the terms of her treaty, especially that clause which secured the English from the supervision of the diabolical Inquisition, and other nations were only waiting an opportunity to draw the sword against her.

Another fleet was consequently fitted out, and Admiral Blake, who had hoisted his flag on board the *Naseby*, sent the summons Lancelot and I had expected to join her.

The admiral looked pale and ill, yet his spirits were as high as ever, and as the fleet sailed down Channel, and the white cliffs of Old England faded from sight, we little thought that he, our beloved chief, had looked his last on the land he loved so dearly.

I can but give a brief account of the important services rendered during the long cruise we had now commenced.

Passing down the coast of Portugal, the admiral sent a frigate up the Tagus, demanding of the King of Portugal a complete fulfilment of the clauses of the late treaty. The effect of the message was satisfactory in the extreme. Every clause was agreed to, and among others the right of Englishmen to have Bibles and Protestant books in their houses, without thereby infringing the laws of the country.

Without stopping we pressed on to Cadiz, looking out for the Silver fleet, which had not arrived.

We here encountered a fearful storm, by which several of our ships were damaged and compelled to return home, but yet the Spaniards would not venture out of port to fight us; and the admiral, leaving Captain Stayner in the *Speaker*, and six other ships to watch in the bay, sailed for Malaga, on which town we inflicted condign punishment in consequence of the assistance the people had afforded to a Genoese and to a Sicilian galley which had taken part with the Spaniards against us.

On our return to Cadiz, we found to our infinite satisfaction that Captain Stayner's squadron had fallen in with the first division of the Silver fleet, and had sunk or captured every galleon containing treasure of immense value.

In the hopes of encountering the second division, the admiral remained at sea the whole winter off Cadiz, notwithstanding the heavy gales we encountered. We were absent from our post a short time, during which we came off Algiers to settle a dispute with the Dey, who, not forgetting the punishment inflicted on Tunis, yielded to our demands without a shot.

On our return towards the Straits, we relieved Tangiers, then a Portuguese settlement, closely invested by the Moors, whom our guns drove away and dispersed. Returning to Cadiz we again endeavoured, but in vain, to draw out the Spanish fleet, and while we lay off and on the harbour, news came from undoubted sources that the second Silver fleet, hearing of the disaster to the first, was afraid of continuing the homeward voyage, and had put into Santa Cruz, a port of one of the Canary Islands.

Thither the admiral resolved to sail with his fleet, now numbering by arrivals from England about twenty-five large ships and frigates.

On the morning of the 19th of April, 1657, the frigate sent on ahead brought intelligence that the Silver fleet, together with several men-of-war and merchant vessels, were at anchor in the bay of Santa Cruz, guarded by castles and batteries of immense strength. Notwithstanding, the wind being favourable, the admiral resolved to attack at once, and the fleet under all sail stood in, Rear-Admiral Stayner, with a portion, being directed to assail the galleons, while the admiral himself assaulted the batteries.

The Spaniards, their ships formed in a semicircle, believing that our defeat was certain, opened a tremendous fire, which every British ship returned with terrible effect to the enemy.

In a few minutes the action became general, equalling in fury any which we had ever fought. So well was our artillery plied, that many of the guns in the castles and batteries were ere long silenced, when, leaving a few frigates to keep them in play, the admiral sailed on to the assistance of the gallant Stayner, and now with our united guns we played havoc among the Spaniards. Ship after ship was set on fire, while two proud galleons had already sunk, and by two o'clock of that eventful day not a mast remained above water—the whole of the Silver fleet was destroyed.

No sooner was the work performed than the wind shifted to the south-west, enabling every one of our ships to sail out again, beyond range of the castle guns. Not one was missing, and we had only fifty men killed and a hundred and fifty wounded in this most gallant exploit.

Some of the most damaged ships were sent home, while we returned to the coast of Spain, where we found the Spaniards eager to make peace in order to avoid future disasters.

Thence we sailed for Salee, to compel the corsairs of that State to restore their Christian captives to freedom. At the appearance of our red-cross banner the Moorish chief sent an envoy on board, promising to comply with all the admiral's demands. In one week every Christian captive in the country was on board our ships. Water and such provisions as we required had been received, and a treaty of peace had been signed, but, alas! we who were with him saw that the admiral's days were numbered.

After looking into the Tagus, our canvas was spread for England. Onwards we pressed under all sail. Often during the voyage he expressed the hope that he might see again his native land. The Lizard was sighted. Soon Ram Head was rounded, and an officer from the deck came into the cabin to announce to us, who with sad hearts were standing round the death-bed of **our** beloved chief, that Plymouth itself was in sight.

Stretching out **his** arms, **he** sought to rise, but his strength had failed. His eyes gazed upwards, his lips murmured a **prayer, and** then, when, from the expression of his noble countenance, **we saw** that his spirit had fled, even the **stoutest - hearted** amongst us **burst** into tears, sobbing like little children. Deep, honest grief was marked **on** the faces of **the** vast crowds which had gathered on the shores to welcome **the returning** hero.

I need not speak **of the** magnificent funeral ordered by the Protector **to** lay **at** rest in Westminster Abbey the **honoured remains of the greatest of** England's admirals.

Among the mourners stood a grey-haired veteran, leaning on a staff to support his tottering steps.

"Alack, alack! Master Ben, it is a sad day, and little did my eyes wish to see it," murmured Martin. "I followed his father to **the grave,** but little did I expect to outlive his noble son. I knows, howsundever, that it won't be for long, and I am ready, **when the Lord** wills, to depart."

Old Martin's words were prophetic. He returned with **Lancelot** and I to Lyme, and in a few days the old sailor **took to his bed, from** which he never rose. We mourned for him sincerely, feeling that we had lost a true and faithful friend. But he was spared from witnessing the degradation of our country.

Three years passed. The great Protector himself was dead. His son had retired into private life, and Charles **Stuart** came back to gain eternal infamy by a thousand vile deeds, not the least among which was to order the body of the great admiral to be exhumed and to be cast into a hole dug near the back door of one of **the** prebendaries of the abbey.

After the death of my patron, I for a short time only went to sea. Dick, who had hitherto remained afloat, came back to be present when Lancelot and I married, and having himself taken a wife, he settled near us in the neighbourhood of Lyme. It was not from lack of my talking of them if our children were not well versed in the deeds of the great admiral which I have briefly narrated in the preceding pages.

THE END.

MOMENTS OF ANXIETY.

THE ORPHANS:

A Tale of the Sea.

BY W. H. G. KINGSTON

THE ORPHANS.

CHAPTER I.

THOSE two were alone in the world — Madeline and her younger brother Hector.

They were orphans. The ship to which their father, Lieutenant Blythe, belonged was lost in a typhoon in the Indian seas, when Hector was a mere child, and their mother had lately been taken from them.

They continued on in the cottage in which they were born on the western coast of Cornwall. The scenery round was wild in the extreme, but they loved it the better for that. Their mother had lived since their father's loss a retired life, devoting herself to their education; and there were no families in the neighbourhood with whom they were intimate.

I have said they were alone in the world; but Jack Twinch would not have allowed, while he held on to life, that such was the case. Jack loved them as if they were his own children. He had been a quartermaster on board the corvette in which their father first went to sea. He had taught the boy, as he often said, to knot and splice, reef and steer, and had done his best to make a sailor of him.

He had, moreover, saved the life of the young midshipman, who had fallen overboard where sharks were swarming; Jack having jumped in and kept the monsters at bay till they were both picked up.

He had afterwards lost a leg, and, being besides severely wounded, was no longer fit to go afloat. He might have borne up for Greenwich, but the lieutenant invited him to stay at his cottage, in Cornwall, as long as he liked. Jack had remained there ever since, employing himself in taking care of the garden, and pigs, and poultry, and cows. Wages he never would receive. He had a small pension, which more than amply supplied all his wants.

Jack Twinch, like many another old sailor, was fond of spinning yarns, and in Hector always found a ready listener. Jack dwelt mostly on the time when Hector's father first went to sea, and delighted in describing his various sayings and gallant doings. He did so without the slightest idea that he was imbuing the boy with an uncontrollable desire to become a sailor.

Hector was sent to school at Bideford, at which place a

large number of his companions were intended for the sea. When he came home for the holidays, his greatest pleasure was to listen to the fresh yarns Jack had to spin, or more frequently to oft-repeated ones about the ocean.

After the death of their mother, Hector had remained at home. Though her children had small pensions, the amount was insufficient to pay for Hector's schooling.

Madeline had, however, various plans for increasing their income, so as to enable him to return to school.

They were one day strolling out together on the wild seashore. They had climbed to a rocky height above the beach, and, sitting down. were watching the ocean spread out before them, now sparkling in the bright light of the evening sun.

Numerous clouds floated across the deep blue sky, their borders tinged with a rich golden hue, while to the southward was gathered a denser mass, against which the wings of the sea-fowl, as they came winging their flight back to their homes amid the cliffs, appeared of snowy whiteness.

Several vessels lay becalmed in the offing. while a steamer was making her way to the southward, closer in shore, bound probably round the Land's End.

Though Madeline had often and often witnessed a similar scene, she could not refrain from exclaiming, " How beautiful ! "

"I wish I was away out there, on board one of those vessels," said Hector. "I ought to be going to sea. Many other fellows of my age are afloat, already making their way up the ratlines."

"Don't talk of it, Hector," said Madeline, her heart sinking within her. "I hope to arrange for you to return to school; then, perhaps, you will be able to go to college, and get some employment on shore, and I will come and live with you, and help you to keep house. There is nothing for you to do near this, or we might be able to live on in the dear old home."

"You are very kind and good, Maddy, and I am grateful; indeed I am," exclaimed Hector. "But there's no use hiding it from you—I shall be miserable if I don't go to sea. I don't care in what way. I would rather serve before the mast on board a collier than not go at all."

"You serve on board a collier!" said Maddy, gazing at the handsome countenance of her much-loved young brother. "Dreadful! you would be sick of the life before you had been many weeks or days on board. I could not bear the thoughts of your going even into the Navy;" and Madeline forthwith began to use every argument she could think of to induce her brother to abandon his purpose.

The more she reasoned with him, the more determined she feared he was to carry out his intention.

At last she gave it up for the present as a hopeless case, and resolved to try what Jack Twinch could do. As they neared their cottage they saw Jack coming to meet them.

"A gentleman has called inquiring for Master Hector, and says he has promised to give him a trip on board the revenue cutter. He's a lieutenant of the Navy, and so I asked him to walk in and sit down, as Master Hector would be at home presently."

"Oh, I know; it must be Lieutenant Lydiard. I met him a few days ago at the coastguard station. He has only lately been appointed, and I told him that we should be very happy to see him if he would look in on us when he came this way."

"How could you think of asking a stranger to the house at this time?" exclaimed Madeline. "However, you must go in and see him while I sit in the garden."

"Oh, yes," answered Hector; "but I may ask him to stop and take tea," and he bounded away before Madeline could reply.

Madeline walked on slowly with Jack, telling him without loss of time what Hector had said to her. "I'd as lief, for your sake and my own, Miss Madeline, that he remained on shore," answered the old sailor; "but to my mind the wish to go to sea is born in him. It is natural like, just as it is for a young duck to take to the water. I'll say what I can, Miss Madeline, but, to tell the truth, it would be against the grain for me to say much about the matter in the way you would wish." Madeline derived very little consolation from her conversation with Jack.

Notwithstanding her disinclination to do the honours of her tea-table to a stranger, prompted by natural curiosity, she at length went into the sitting-room, where she found her brother and his visitor. The latter rose, begging Hector to introduce him.

He was a young man with handsome features and an exceedingly pleasing expression of countenance. He apologised for calling at so late an hour, excusing himself on the plea that he had promised to give his young friend a trip on board the revenue cutter, which would call off the shore for him the following morning.

"You won't mind me going, Madeline, will you?" exclaimed Hector.

"Perhaps, Miss Blythe, you may be tempted to come yourself, if you consider your brother a sufficient escort," said the lieutenant.

Madeline declined, but did not object to Hector's going, provided he could be landed again before nightfall.

In common courtesy, Madeline felt herself compelled to invite the lieutenant to remain for tea. Though young, he had been on several foreign stations; and when he at length took his departure, Madeline had to confess that he was very agreeable.

The next morning he called to take Hector off, promising to bring him back in good time.

Madeline was well accustomed to be left alone, and always found plenty of occupation. She had another talk with Jack about her brother, but it ended much as the former had done; and she began to fear that she should find no one to assist her in weaning Hector from his desire to go to sea.

In the evening Lieutenant Lydiard again appeared with Hector. Madeline felt compelled to ask him to remain to tea. He might, perhaps, assist her in persuading Hector not to go to sea.

While her brother was out of the room, she told her guest of her difficulties on the subject.

" I would not have asked him to take a trip with us had I known your wishes," answered the lieutenant; "but I will try in future to make him understand the little chance there is of a youngster without interest getting on in the service. Were I to speak of the dangers and hardships he must look for, that would have little effect with a lad of spirit."

After this the lieutenant became a very frequent visitor at the cottage; and though Madeline had first wondered why he came so often, she at length began to suspect the cause, and acknowledged even to herself that she should have been disappointed had he passed by without calling.

The lieutenant had always some excuse for looking in. Generally he called to see Hector, who was always ready to accompany him to the stations it was his duty to visit. He was not very successful in persuading his young friend to follow Madeline's wishes.

Hector argued that many who had entered the Navy with no more interest than he possessed had risen to the highest rank, and why should not he?

"The chances are you do not," said the lieutenant.

" But there are chances that I shall," answered Hector, "and I intend to try. If I don't succeed I shan't be worse off probably than if I remain on shore."

To this remark the lieutenant had nothing to say. It did not occur to him to tell Hector that it was his duty to remain and take care of his sister, or that argument might have had more influence than any of those he had used. Madeline was too unselfish to employ it herself, and

Hector every day became more fixed in his resolution. Had he been at school, he would have had less time to think about the matter.

All Jack could say had no effect; indeed, the boy always turned the arguments he used against him.

Hector was continually talking on the subject, though he showed some consideration for his sister by planning what she should do during his absence.

Month after month went by, but nothing was arranged. Lieutenant Lydiard wrote to several friends, but their answers were unsatisfactory. At length one day he called, and drawing an official-looking despatch from his pocket, told Madeline that he brought news which pained him much, though it under other circumstances would have been highly gratifying.

"I have been appointed," he said, "as first lieutenant of the *Orion* frigate, destined for the East India station, and she may be kept there for three or four years. I should be shelved entirely were I to refuse to go. My only satisfaction will be if I can obtain a berth for your brother on board her."

Madeline felt her heart sink as the lieutenant was speaking. He said no more. Madeline expected that he would have spoken a word she hoped to hear, and her feelings told her that she should not have refused.

He looked very unhappy, and several times he appeared as if about to speak, but by an effort he restrained himself.

Hector was full of gratitude for Mr. Lydiard's promise,

and fully believed that his long-cherished wishes were at length to be gratified.

The lieutenant was gone. Madeline believed that he would write. She was sure he would about Hector; but day after day passed by and no letter came from him. Poor Madeline felt her heart grow sick; Hector was well-nigh in despair. He consulted Jack as to what he should do.

Jack feared that something might have happened to the lieutenant, for he was sure that he was not a man who was likely to prove false.

At length Madeline received a letter. He addressed her as "My dear Miss Blythe." It was full of regrets at having been unable to obtain a berth for her brother. He had been compelled to leave his ship to attend to the funeral of his father, and every moment of his time since his return had been occupied. He had put off writing, in the hopes of having some satisfactory intelligence to send. The frigate was on the point of sailing, but he had written to the Admiralty and to all the friends he possessed urging Hector's claims, and he trusted that she might hear from some of them before long. Only one short sentence made her believe that the lieutenant's heart was hers.

Hector could scarcely refrain from bursting into tears when Madeline read the letter to him. His hopes revived, however, when she suggested that some of the friends Lieutenant Lydiard spoke of might remember his wishes.

Hector appeared doomed to be disappointed. Week after week passed away, and no letter came to tell him that he was appointed to a ship. Madeline saw that some steps must be taken, as he was sadly idling away his time.

They were talking over the matter one evening, and Hector expressed his readiness to do whatever she wished, when a loud peal of thunder announced that a storm had broken. The windows began to rattle, and the increasing roar of the surf showed that the wind was blowing on the shore.

"It will be a bad look-out for any vessels which fail to get a good offing before nightfall," observed Hector.

"I trust the signs of the coming gale were seen in good time by any vessels off the coast," said Madeline.

Hector went to the front door, which he could with difficulty close behind him after he had opened it.

"I fancied I heard a gun fired," he said, on his return; "but the wind howls so loudly among the trees that I could scarcely distinguish any other sounds." He went into the kitchen to ask old Jack his opinion. Hector found him putting on his sou'wester and flushing coat. He too had heard not only one but several guns, and was bent upon going down to the shore.

Hector was quickly ready to accompany him. They called on the way at the cottage of a fisherman who, with his son, agreed to go with them and to carry some ropes and spars, in case the ship in distress should drive on shore. They carried a lantern also, and a couple of torches, with which they could form a bright light, should it be necessary to guide any boat or raft coming from the wreck, for that

the craft whose guns they had heard would be wrecked
they felt sure. Their worst fears were realised. As they
reached the beach, a flash of lightning revealed to them a
large brig with her mainmast gone driving in towards the
rocks. At that instant her anchor was let go.

CHAPTER II.

FEAR it won't hold her long," exclaimed Jack.

He was right. In a few minutes the cable parted, and again she drove towards the reef. Her boats apparently had been washed away, for none were lowered. Her fate was sealed. She struck on the outer edge of the reef, and a sea swept across her decks.

Hector and his companions hurried along the beach to get abreast of the vessel.

"If any one comes ashore, it will be hereabouts," said Jack.

They lighted one of the torches to show the shipwrecked crew that friends were ready to assist them.

"When they see this they'll try to send a line on shore with a float," said Jack.

They waded into the surf as far as they could venture,

in the hopes of discovering the float. Presently Hector cried out, " I see a man. Fasten the rope round my waist, and I'll get hold of him." Not a moment was to be lost. Young as he was, he was a bold swimmer, and dashing fearlessly into the sea, he made towards the person he had seen. Grasping him tightly, they were both hauled up together.

The man he had saved was so exhausted as to be unable to speak. While old Jack was trying to recover him, Hector and the fishermen again went down to the water. but no attempt was made from the vessel to open a communication with the shore.

In a short time two seamen were washed on the beach, but they were corpses. In vain Hector and his companions waited ; not another living being came on shore. While they were watching the vessel, she lifted from off the reef where she had first struck and drove close into the rocks, when the moon rising above the cliff revealed her position clearly to view. They shouted at the top of their voices, but no answer came. It was evident that the crew had been washed from the deck when she first struck.

On rejoining Jack, they found that he had failed in his efforts to restore the stranger to consciousness. From his dress they judged that he was the captain or mate of the vessel.

" We must have him up to the house, and see what we can do for him there," said Jack. " Miss Madeline will be willing, I am sure."

They formed a litter of the spars and ropes, and bore the

shipwrecked man along. Jack had him placed in his bed, and Madeline and her young maid-servant quickly got ready such restoratives as they knew were required. They proved efficacious, and by the next morning the stranger was so far recovered as to be able to state that he was Captain Durell, master of the *Good Intent* brig, from the West Indies bound to Bristol; that he had met with much bad weather, and his mainmast having been sprung had been carried away, when the gale caught him close in with the land. He with the rest had been washed from the deck, but being a good swimmer he had managed to keep afloat till rescued by Hector.

"You saved my life, young gentleman, and I am grateful," he added.

Captain Durell had suffered more than he had at first supposed. For three days he was unable to leave his bed, and was even then not in a fit state to travel. Madeline begged that he would remain till he was perfectly recovered.

Hector was frequently with him, and did not fail to speak of his desire to go to sea.

"As my brig was lost through no fault of mine, I expect to get command of another vessel before long. If you wish it, I will gladly take you with me," he said. "You shall live in my cabin; and as soon as you have gained a due knowledge of seamanship and can pass your examination, I will ensure you being made a mate."

Hector answered that it was above all things what he desired, as he had no chance of entering the Navy.

Captain Durell had saved a purse of gold, and he offered a handsome present to Hector, who, however, at once declined it, and Madeline much approved of his having done so.

In about ten days Captain Durell took his departure, his last words to Hector being, " I will not forget my promise to you."

Within a month after this Hector received a letter from Captain Durell, who said that he had got the command of a fine new ship, and invited him to come forthwith to Bristol. He was to bring nothing with him, as his entire outfit would be provided. A sum of money was also enclosed for his journey.

" You'll not ask me to refuse," exclaimed Hector, as he placed the letter in his sister's hands.

It cost Madeline much to give her consent; but Jack pleaded for Hector. Captain Durell had gained his confidence; " and it was his belief," he said, " that Hector might never have so good an opportunity. The captain was his friend, and would do his utmost to promote his interests."

Hector's box, with a few things he had to carry, was packed up. Jack accompanied him to the place where the coach for Bristol passed by.

Hector promised to write very often. When he was gone, Madeline, who had hitherto borne up, burst into tears. Hector's first letter somewhat consoled her. He was delighted with his ship, the *Glenalvon*. Captain Durell was as kind to him as if he were his son. They were bound out for the West Indies, and he hoped to be back again in about six months, " and after that we shall perhaps be sent to India or Australia," he added.

Hector gave numerous other details; indeed, he had never before written so long a letter. Another came, entrusted to the pilot as the ship was leaving the river, in which he expressed himself equally well satisfied with everything as at first.

Months passed by after this, and Madeline did not hear from her brother. She had hoped that Lieutenant Lydiard would, as he had promised, write to Hector; but day after day the postman passed her door. She began to fear that the lieutenant had forgotten his promise, and then that something dreadful must have happened to Hector; perhaps that the *Glenalvon* had been overtaken by one of those hurricanes of which she had so often read as occurring in the West Indies, and that her young brother was lost. Her heart sank within her.

Old Jack did his best to comfort her. " Perhaps the owners had sent the *Glenalvon* on a longer voyage than was first intended. Hector had very likely written and his letter miscarried. The return of ships to port was always uncertain. Cheer up, Miss Madeline," he added; " we shall see the boy back again, never fear." Still Madeline could not recover her spirits. Had Ralph Lydiard written, she might have done so, but everything around her wore a sombre hue. She had no female correspondents, no friends who could sympathise with her. She felt herself more than ever alone in the world.

Occasionally the wife of a farmer in the neighbourhood sent her in a newspaper, which afforded her some amusement, and she now eagerly scanned its pages in search of shipping news.

One day her eye was caught by the name of the *Glenalvon*, which, after encountering heavy weather, had arrived safely at Bristol. She would now without fail hear from Hector. She in vain waited. At last she wrote to the owners.

They replied that her brother, with the captain and several of the crew, had been left on shore at Jamaica, ill with the yellow fever when the ship sailed.

"He is among strangers, without any one to nurse him," exclaimed Madeline.

She determined at once to go to Bristol, and according to the information she should there obtain to proceed out to the West Indies. Jack wished to accompany her, but she begged him not to think of it. The expense would be greater than she could afford, and he must stop at home to take care of the house. Should she find Hector sufficiently recovered to make the voyage, she would bring him at once to England.

Old Jack was ready to do whatever she desired. She set off by herself. The owners of the *Glenalvon* received her politely. They had another ship about to sail with several lady passengers. There was one cabin vacant, which was at her service. She immediately engaged it.

It was the first time Madeline had been at sea since she had accompanied her father on a short trip from Portsmouth to Plymouth. She loved the ocean, much cause as she had to dread it.

She soon got accustomed to the life on board; yet even here she felt herself alone. The ladies had their families to attend to, and generally retired early to their berths. It was her delight to walk the deck when the sun had gone down and the moon came forth, and its beams sparkled on the calm waters.

The ship was wafted along by a favourable breeze, and the weather long continued fine. Madeline's mind naturally was constantly dwelling on her young brother, and perhaps, too, on another, far away. Earnestly she prayed that they might be preserved.

One evening she stopped in her walk and leant over the bulwarks, with her hands clasped, in the attitude of prayer, and fervently she prayed that all might go well.

The ship was approaching her destination. In a few days she would see her brother, or learn if he had succumbed to the fearful fever. Her heart sank within her. "Alas, alas! I dread the worst," she said to herself. It seemed to her that voices were wafted from afar, across the ocean, and she fancied that she heard the words, "Be not faithless, but trust to Him who made this mighty sea, and orders all for the best."

She remained thus she knew not how long, till she heard a footstep near her, and the captain said, "Let me advise you, Miss Blythe, to retire to your cabin, or we shall have you on the sick list before we reach Jamaica. The moon is said to play curious pranks in these latitudes."

She aroused herself, and followed the well-intentioned advice. The wind continued light, and it was not till three days afterwards that the ship entered Kingston Harbour.

The first person who came on board was Captain Durell. Madeline trembled with anxiety as she hurried up to him.

"Where is Hector?" she asked, gazing into the captain's face. "Why has he not come with you?"

"He would have done so, but he is with some friends a few miles up the country," he answered. "I will send a messenger for him, and he will soon be here."

Madeline burst into tears. They were tears of joy. Within a few hours Hector was receiving his sister's loving embrace. He had made the friendship of a planter's family, who received Madeline with great kindness and begged her to stay with them while she remained on the island.

Captain Durell, however, was soon again to sail in command of the *Glenalvon*, the master who had brought her out having died. He, of course, wished to take Hector with him, and he offered Madeline a passage home.

Once more Madeline was at sea. The voyage commenced favourably, and she looked forward with satisfaction to the thoughts of returning to her own quiet home.

Hector confessed that, though he had no reason to complain of the merchant service, he would much rather have entered the Navy. He had been on board two or three ships of war in Port Royal Harbour, and had found some of his father's old messmates, who had treated him with much kindness.

"I still hope that some of Lieutenant Lydiard's friends may succeed in getting me appointed to a ship," he added.

The *Glenalvon* had got into mid-ocean when the weather changed, and instead of the light winds which had hitherto wafted her along, a heavy gale sprang up, and the sea rose into mountain billows. Madeline wished to witness the ocean in its fury, but Hector urged her to remain below, for the sea was breaking over the deck, and it was impossible to say what might next happen. As night drew on the weather became even worse. A fearful crash was heard, and the voice of the captain reached Madeline's ears, ordering the crew to clear the wreck of the mainmast. Madeline anxiously waited the appearance of Hector to tell her what had happened, but he did not come, and she trembled lest some accident should have happened to him. The black steward at last entered the cabin. "Three men," he said, "have been washed overboard, and the ship is in a dangerous state."

"Where is my brother?" she asked in a trembling voice.

"He is on deck, attending to his duty," was the answer.

Shortly afterwards another crash came. The foremast had been carried away. The mizenmast soon shared the same fate, and the *Glenalvon* lay a helpless hulk on the troubled ocean.

The night wore on. A clanking sound was heard. It was that of the pumps, and it went on without cessation.

At length Madeline's chief anxiety was relieved by seeing Hector. He looked pale and fatigued.

"The ship is in a bad way. I must not conceal it from you," he said. "I have been relieved from my spell at pumps, but I shall soon have to take another turn. Do all we can, it's a hard matter to keep the ship afloat; but if the gale abates we may get at the leak and stop it, and then rig jurymasts."

Hector was not allowed long rest. All hands were required to labour at the pumps. Thus the night passed away, tho morning brought no abatement of the storm. The officers and crew worked for their lives, but with all their exertions the leak continued to gain on them.

The boats had been destroyed by the fall of the masts, and unless the ship could be kept afloat they must perish.

When for a short time Hector was allowed to rest, he returned to the cabin.

."I'll come to you when all hope is gone, that we may die together, Madeline," he said. "Pray for yourself and us. We have still two hours of daylight, and perhaps before dark a sail may heave in sight and take us off; but the captain does not believe that we can keep the ship afloat another night, though the wind has decreased and the sea has somewhat gone down."

When Hector next entered the cabin, overcome by fatigue, he sank down by the side of Madeline on the sofa to which she was clinging.

"Is the leak still gaining on us?" she asked.

"Yes; slowly but surely," answered her brother.

"Nothing but a miracle can save us. I grieve to tell you so, but we must look our position in the face."

"We will pray," said Madeline, and she knelt down on the deck of the cabin. She had been in this attitude for some minutes when a cry was heard, "A sail! a sail!"

It restored vigour to the arms of the well-nigh exhausted crew, and they worked away with greater energy than ever at the pumps. Hector returned on deck to labour with the rest. Still they had long to wait. The sail was made out to be a British man-of-war, a corvette. She passed under the stern of the sinking ship and hove to, to leeward. A boat was lowered and approached. Hector rushed into the cabin. "Come, Madeline!" he exclaimed. "The captain says that you and I, as the youngest, must go first; and he will allow no man to enter the boat till we are safe in her."

Madeline accompanied her brother on deck. The only way to reach the boat was by springing from the main chains.

Captain Durell stood by to direct them, and to keep his crew back. Ready arms were in the boat stretched out to receive them. Hector took his sister round the waist.

"Now!" exclaimed the captain, as the boat was lifted close to the chains; and they were both in another instant on board and uninjured.

The youngest mate and three other men alone were allowed to follow them. The rest were still working at the pumps. The boat returned to the corvette. To reach her deck was a dangerous operation; but ropes were lowered, and Madeline and Hector were drawn up in safety.

The gallant boat's crew then returned to the rescue of the remainder of the people on board the ship. Madeline, overcome by the alarming anxiety she had gone through, would have sunk on the deck had not the commander of the corvette, who was standing ready, supported her. She gazed up in his countenance. That glance told her he was Lieutenant Lydiard.

"Thank heaven you are preserved, Madeline," he said, as he carried her, followed by Hector, to his cabin.

She happily did not hear the cry which rose from the crew of the corvette, as ere the boat had got many fathoms away from her side, the ship with all on board was seen to go down.

The boat pulled on, but the distance between the vessels had been greatly increased, and before the spot where she sunk was reached, the water had washed over the heads of all who had been on board. Some days passed before Madeline was told of the sad occurrence.

The corvette was on her homeward voyage, and Lieutenant Lydiard, who had gained great credit for several gallant actions while in the Indian seas, having been promoted, commanded her. At his request, Hector, whose name had long been down at the Admiralty, was appointed midshipman to a ship then fitting out. He no longer hesitated to offer his hand to Madeline.

She, soon after the ship was paid off, became his wife.

Hector by his strict attention to the call of duty, and by the courage and intelligence he had frequent opportunities

of exhibiting, notwithstanding his want of interest, rose in
the service, and Jack Twinch lived to see him in command
of a fine corvette, on board which Captain Lydiard's eldest
boy first went to sea.

THE END.